In praise of *The Book of God*

A worthy and highly laudable version of the greatest story ever told.

Isabel Anders, *A Closer Look*

Walter Wangerin Jr. has accomplished a feat of imagination and faith.

Philip Yancey, award-winning author

Walter Wangerin Jr. releases our imaginations to take in all the color, texture, and grit implicit in the biblical story and engages us as fresh and astonished participants.

Eugene H. Peterson

Walter Wangerin Jr. is a very good writer . . . a skilled and original teller of tales.

Thomas Howard

Wangerin has made the Bible exciting. I knew most of the stories and yet I was hard-pressed to put it down.

Curt Schleier, *The Detroit Free Press*

Wangerin gives personality and warmth to biblical figures. . . . Wangerin seeks to recapture the Bible as a story of relationships between an eternal God and ordinary men and women.

David Briggs, AP News Service

Walter Wangerin Jr. has done us a great service by breathing life into the pages of the Old and New Testaments.

Benjamin S. Carson, Sr., MD,
Johns Hopkins University Hospital

For those who desire a novelist's different perspective on some very familiar stories, Wangerin is likely to be a welcome voice.

Whether the stories are familiar from childhood or encountered here for the first time, you will be struck by their palpable power.... The experience is exhilarating.

The Book of God comes as a refreshing way of encouraging readers of all ages to get acquainted and reacquainted with the world's most remarkable book.

THE
BOOK
OF
GENESIS

Other books by Walter Wangerin Jr.

The Book of God: The Bible as a Novel
Little Lamb, Who Made Thee?
Mourning into Dancing
Reliving the Passion
The Orphean Passages
Ragman and Other Cries of Faith
The Manger Is Empty
Miz Lil and the Chronicles of Grace
The Book of the Dun Cow
The Book of Sorrows

THE

A Selection from the
Best-selling The Book of God

BOOK

OF

Walter Wangerin Jr.

GENESIS

The Ancient Generations

ZondervanPublishingHouse
Grand Rapids, Michigan

A Division of HarperCollins*Publishers*

The Book of Genesis
Copyright © 1997, 1996 by Walter Wangerin Jr.

Parts One and Two of this book are extracted from *The Book of God: The Bible as a Novel*, copyright © 1996 by Walter Wangerin Jr.

Requests for information should be addressed to:

ZondervanPublishingHouse
Grand Rapids, Michigan 49530

Wangerin, Walter.
    [Book of God. Selections]
    The book of Genesis : a selection from the best-selling The Book of God / Walter Wangerin, Jr.
        p.   cm.
    ISBN 0-310-21791-1 (pbk.)
    1. Bible. O.T. Genesis—History of Biblical events—Fiction.   I. Title.
PS3573.A477B552   1997
813'.54—dc21   97–1883
                                                   CIP

Published in association with the literary agency of Alive Communications, 1465 Kelly Johnson Blvd., Suite 320, Colorado Springs, CO 80920, and in cooperation with Lion Publishing, Oxford, England.

Printed in the United States of America

97 98 99 00 01 02 03 04 /❖ OP/ 10 9 8 7 6 5 4

Now comes Ezra the priest down from the old palace mount, carrying the scrolls in his arms. He enters the square before the Water Gate and passes through a great congregation of people all sitting on the ground.

At the far end they have constructed a wooden platform. They've built a pulpit for this reading.

Ezra ascends the platform, steps to the front, and unrolls the scrolls.

Spontaneously the people rise up

Ezra blesses the Lord. All the people raise their hands and answer, "Amen!" "Amen!"

And then, when they've sat down again, Ezra the priest begins to read.

"In the beginning God created the heavens and the earth.

"The earth was without form and void, and darkness was upon the face of the deep; and the Spirit of God was moving over the face of the waters.

"And God said, 'Let there be light.'

"And there was light."

CONTENTS

✠

Part I
The Family

✣

ABRAHAM

1

An old man entered his tent, dropping the door flap behind him. In the darkness he knelt slowly before a clay firepot, very tired. He blew on a coal until it glowed, then he bore the spark to the wick of a saucer lamp. It made a soft nodding flame. The man's face was lean and wounded and streaked with the dust of recent travel. He began to unroll a straw mat for sleeping but paused halfway, lost in thought.

Altogether the tent was rectangular, sewn of goatskins and everywhere patched with fresher skins of the goat. Across the middle a reed screen hung from three poles, dividing the space into two compartments, one for the man, one for his wife. These two were all that dwelt in the tent. There were neither children nor grandchildren. There never had been.

A vagrant wind slapped the side of the tent so that it billowed inward, but the man didn't move. He was gazing into the finger-flame of the lamp.

Old man. Perhaps eighty years old. Nevertheless, this present weariness did not come from age. In fact, the man had a small wiry body as light and as tough as leather. Nor was his eye diminished. It watched with a steadfast grey light, awaiting interpretation. It was not an old eye, but a patient one.

Not age, then. Rather, the man was made weary by this day's travel and yesterday's war.

His only relative in the entire land of Canaan—even from the Euphrates River in the east to the Nile in Egypt—was a nephew who had chosen the easier life. Though the old man himself lived in tents, Lot, his nephew, dwelt in the cities of the Jordan valley, the watered places, fertile places, desirable, sweet and green. But lately four kings of the north had attacked and defeated five cities of the valley. One of these was Sodom, the city Lot had chosen. Among the prisoners whom the northern kings carried away, then, was Lot.

As soon as the old man heard that his kinsman had been taken captive, he armed three hundred and eighteen of his own men, mounted donkeys, and pursued the enemy with a light and secret speed. In the night he divided his forces. He surprised the northern kings by striking from two sides at once. He routed them. He drove them home. And all their plunder, all their prisoners he brought back to the cities that had been defeated: Sodom, Gomorrah, Admah, Zeboiim, Zoar. Lot was free again, and again he chose Sodom for his dwelling—though the men of the place had a reputation for extreme wickedness.

That was yesterday.

Today the king of Sodom had offered the old man all the plunder he'd returned, but the old man refused.

Today the Priest-King Melchizedek had come forth with bread and wine to honor the old man, and he honored him saying:

> Blessed are you!
> Blessed, too, be the God most high
> who delivers your foe into your hand!

And today the old man had come back to his tents, again, near the oaks of Mamre, tired.

Today, in the evening, his wife had baked him a barley cake, though he ate scarcely anything and she herself ate nothing at all.

"Is the young man safe, then?" she had asked.

"Yes," he told her.

"And his children?" she said, looking dead level at her husband. "How are the children of the man who lives within the walls of houses?"

"Safe," said the man.

"They are home, then?" she said. "Lot sits contented among his children, then? Lot looks upon the consolation of his old age, then, because he has an uncle who saves him when his own choices get him into trouble?"

The old man said nothing.

"Because he has a good uncle?" she continued. "A generous uncle? An uncle whose wife never did put the first bite of barley cake into the mouth of her own child?"

It was then that the old man arose and left his food unfinished. He trudged through the dusk to his own side of the tent and entered and pulled the flap down behind him-self and lit the lamp and fell to staring at the single flame, the straw mat only half unrolled in front of him. He was very tired. He was kneeling, sitting back on his heels. He maintained that same posture, unwinking, unsleeping, through the entire first watch of the night. All sound had long since ceased outside. The encampment slept. His wife, finally, had fallen asleep on the other side of the reed screen. She was sleeping alone.

Then, in the middle of that night, God spoke.

Fear not, Abram, God said, calling the old man by name. I am your shield. Your reward shall be very great.

Abram did not move. He did not so much as shift his eye from the orange lamp-flame. But his jaw tightened.

God said, Abram, northward of this place, southward and eastward and westward—all the land as far as
you can see I will give to you and to your descendants
forever.

Still motionless and so softly that the wind outside
concealed the sound of it even from his own ears, Abram
breathed these words: "So you have said. So you have
said. But what, O Lord God, can you give us as long as
we continue childless?"

A wind took hold of the tentflap and lifted it like a
linen. The lamp-flame guttered and went out.

God said, Come. Abram, come outside.

On his hands and knees the old man obeyed.

God said, Raise your eyes to heaven. Look to the
stars, Abram. Count them. Can you count them?

The old man said, "No. I cannot count them. They
are too many."

Even so many, said the Lord God, shall be your
descendants upon the earth.

With the same gaze as he had earlier turned upon
the lamp-flame Abram gazed toward heaven. Now there
was no wind at all. The air was absolutely still. Nothing
moved in the land, except that the man could hear the
sighing of his old wife inside her compartment.

He said, "Is it required then that a slave born within
my household must be my heir?"

God said, Your own son shall be your heir.

Abram said, "How shall I know that? How can I
know, when you have given us no offspring?"

Then the word of the Lord came to the old man.

Abram? said God. Have you seen how a king will by
a covenant establish his promise with his servant?
Tomorrow, Abram. Tomorrow prepare the beasts. I am
the Lord who brought you here to give you this land.

Tomorrow I will make my covenant with you—and thereby shall you surely know my promises to you!

On the following morning the old man rose early. Without an explanation to any in the household, neither to his wife nor to his servants, he took from his herds a heifer, a she-goat, and a ram, all three years old, a turtle-dove, and a young pigeon.

These beasts he led to high ground, to a bare and lonely place where he tethered them.

Abram bound his robe to his waist and the sleeves to his elbows so that nothing hung loosely. He took a long copper knife and with quick cuts to either side of their necks he slaughtered the animals. They sank down and died without protesting. Then the old man drove the knife into the heifer at the top of her breastbone. Mightily he yanked the blade downward, cracking bone, slicing flesh, and cutting the carcass into two separate parts. He did the same for the goat and for the ram, though he did not cut the birds in two.

The halves of each animal Abram laid on the ground opposite each other, creating, as it were, a pathway up through the center of their bodies.

By late afternoon blood and the raw meat had drawn birds of prey to the sky above this lonely place. They circled lower and lower on watchful wings. Finally, in their hunger they dropped and tried to land. But Abram ran at them, shouting and waving his arms. The old man exhausted himself that day, driving the great raptor birds back from the carrion, protecting the animals of the covenant of God.

But then as the sun was going down it was more than mere weariness that came upon him. A deep sleep seized

Abram. Dread and a marvelous darkness swept over him, and he sank to the ground, helpless.

When the sun was altogether gone and the whole world had descended into perfect night, there came a smoking firepot sailing through the dark—a furnace of smoke and a flaming torch. As they passed between the halves of the animals, the Lord God made a covenant with Abram, saying, To your descendants I give this land, from the river of Egypt to the great river, the river Euphrates, the land of the Kenites, the Kenizzites, the Kadmonites, the Hittites, the Perizzites, the Rephaim, the Amorites, the Canaanites, the Girgashites and the Jebusites.

When Abram returned to his tents the following day, he bathed himself carefully and buried his clothes.

But he told no one where he had gone or what he had done or why he'd come back caked with dried blood.

2

Sarai, for her part, was even more anxious than her husband regarding the promises of God. Abram had already entered his eighty-fifth year, and she herself was seventy-five.

And lo, O Lord: we are as childless as the day you first gave hope to my husband and me!

That hope had been planted a full ten years ago. Sarai was intensely aware of time. She had suffered the passage of every barren month since the coming of the promises of God. For the Lord had said to Abram, I will make of you a great nation. But a nation begins with the birth of one child.

Where is this child? Often the old woman placed her hands upon her sunken belly and thought, Where is my child?

Sarai admitted that she had been unrestrained in laughter and dancing when the Lord God interrupted their quiet lives. It became the gossip of their city—"Old Sarai thinks she will bear a baby yet!"—and it might have been an embarrassment to Abram, if he had not already planned to leave.

They were living in Haran at the time, far to the north of this dry place, on the river Balik. Not in tents, in houses. Family and friends surrounded them, and though they were childless, by the time Abram was in his seventies they seemed content. Long ago Sarai had ceased to speak of children. She sincerely believed that she had accepted her sad fate.

But one night Abram came and woke her, his face ashen, his eyes smoky and enormous, his voice ghostly.

"Sarai, Sarai," he whispered, "prepare to leave."

"Leave? Where? Is your father sick again?"

Terah was failing in those years, often calling his son to his side.

Abram did not acknowledge the question. He looked like a blackened candle wick, rigid and breakable. "The Lord God has commanded me to go to a land which he will show me. Sarai," the man said, his voice issuing from his throat like wind from a cave, "he has made marvelous promises. He says he will make of me a great nation, and bless me, and make my name great so that I will be a blessing. I will bless those who bless you, he said. And him who curses you I will curse. By you all the families of the earth shall bless themselves. Sarai, get ready. We've got to go—"

And then when Abram had departed into the night, Sarai began to pant. She bowed her head and covered her face with both hands and burst into tears. A great nation starts with a single child!

Sarai, Abram's wife, was going to have a baby.

She could scarcely stand the sweetness low in her womb. A baby! Let people gossip about her strange behavior, her impossible expectations. Nothing bothered Sarai now.

Indeed, she traveled from Haran without complaint—she and Abram and his nephew Lot, their servants and their cattle. No matter that no one knew where they were going. The God of her husband was leading them. And a glad anticipation made the old woman young again. Blood flowed brightly in Sarai's face. No matter that they now became wanderers living in tents. No matter that, when Abram and his nephew had to divide their flocks and families, Lot chose houses in the cities of the Jordan valley, while her husband continued to roam in tents. None of this mattered—because she had received the promise of God: she who had been barren was about to bear a baby.

But that was ten years ago.

And the bloom had long since faded in Sarai's face.

Moreover, womanhood was as dead as leather within her, and the miracle itself seemed a withered thing now.

Yet God had aroused the desire inside of Sarai, and it would not lie down and die again. Every night it plucked at her heart: Where is it? Where is the child of my own womb? No, Sarai could never again be content with her fate—not after laughter and dancing and trust and all the changes the promise had caused in her life.

Therefore, she took matters into her own hands.

Sarai remembered a custom of Haran, a certain way by which to solve the problem of a woman's barrenness. Perhaps Abram had left most of his past in that land, but the promises of his God must not be left behind, so neither would Sarai leave behind this final chance for a child of her own.

"Abram?" she said. "I have an idea."

They were sitting outside and eating supper several days after he had returned all bloody from some private ceremony. He had not explained the blood and she hadn't asked. They were in the latter part of the meal. Sarai had cut a melon into parts for him, and he was eating them slowly.

"What is your idea?" he said.

She cast her eyes to the side, now cutting melon for herself. "I would not object," she said, "if you liked my idea and acted upon it. Another woman might object. I would not. In fact, I would be grateful."

Abram put a sticky finger to his tongue. "What is your idea?" he said.

"You know my maidservant, of course," she said, carefully cutting the rind from her fruit.

"Yes."

"Hagar. The sturdy woman whom we brought north from Egypt. That one. Young, she is. A good servant."

"Yes," said Abram. "I know her. What is your idea?"

"Now, then, are you finished with the melon? Have you had enough?"

Abram simply sat and gazed at his wife.

Finally she laid the pieces of her own fruit aside and wiped her hands and folded them in her lap and lifted her eyes to her husband.

"When certain wives are unable to bear children," she said, "they bring their maidservants to their husbands.

They invite their husbands to go in to their maidservants in order that they, the barren wives, might in this manner get children of their own. For if the maid bears a baby upon the knees of her mistress, the baby becomes the child of the mistress. Abram, if you wished to do such a thing with Hagar my maidservant . . . I would not object."

For a long time the old man continued to gaze at the old woman. She lowered her eyes.

"It was just an idea," she said.

Abram said, "Bring her to me," and he rose and retired to his room in the tent.

Hagar the Egyptian was not pretty. But Sarai always declared her handsome. She'd chosen this one in the first place because she had large hands and large feet, strength, bones like tent stakes. Only recently had Sarai also noted the generous width of Hagar's hips. Room. Wide black eyes, a broad forehead, not much learning, of course—but room.

On the morning after Hagar slept in Abram's compartment, Sarai saw for the first time that Hagar's hair was long and glossy and raven-black. One might call it beautiful. That same morning she commanded her maidservant to cut her hair short. "It has always interfered with your work," she said.

And then she saw that Hagar her maidservant had conceived. The Egyptian's complexion glowed so dark and fiercely that her eyes and teeth were a shock of whiteness. And when she began to show her teeth more and more in smiling, Sarai knew of a certainty that Hagar, too, knew a baby lay in her womb.

Soon another sign proved both Hagar's pregnancy and her awareness: she swaggered. Distinctly, she began to throw her hips left and right when she walked; and she began to look her mistress dead-level in the eyes; and she simply did not do the things Sarai commanded her to do. She never did get around to cutting her hair.

Sarai said, "Hagar, you go and draw the water this morning." But Hagar sighed and said she was tired, turned on her heel, went to Abram's side of the tent, sat down and ate figs.

And grew huge.

One day Sarai and a midwife were demonstrating how a maid might bear the babe on the knees of her mistress. The older woman made a roll of her sleeping mat and reclined against it, her legs thrust straight before her; Hagar sat on Sarai's thighs, leaning back on the old woman's breast, drawing her own legs up as high as she could; the midwife crouched over Sarai's ankles and faced Hagar, reaching down between Hagar's thighs.

"You see?" said Sarai. "The child will come out on my knees. I'll wrap my arms around you, Hagar, and press down on your belly like this—"

Hagar cried out and slapped Sarai's hands. "That hurts," she said. She stood up and swaggered out of the tent. Sarai sat stunned. The midwife lowered her face and said nothing.

On the following day, Sarai found Hagar sitting in the shade of Abram's tent with a bowl of figs.

Sarai stood above her. "You struck me," she said.

Hagar said, "Yes, and I told the master, your husband, that I was sorry. So I am sorry. And I told him, too, that you didn't mean to hurt me. It's just that I am soft and you are bony. I think he understands the difference, don't you? I said that maybe I am tender now because I am in the way of women, and that maybe you are rough because you are not."

Sarai opened her mouth to answer but groaned instead—a humiliating sound. So then she shouted her words: "It's your turn to . . . get water—"

Hagar said, "I'm sorry. Your husband commanded me to rest. I am obeying Abram."

The next time that Sarai sought to practice the bearing of this infant upon her knees, Hagar said, "Perhaps that won't be necessary anymore."

Straightway Sarai gathered her robe and, like a storm arising from the sea, she went in search of Abram.

This was a country of high grassy hills from which one could see many miles around. Sarai climbed a bald knoll and shaded her eyes and looked for the flocks of her husband, and then for the colors of his garments. He would be among shepherds today, choosing a lamb with which to trade for a particular luxury in the cities: a baby cradle.

There he was. There was Abram.

Even before she had reached the valley of his flocks, Sarai yelled, "Old man! Old man! May the wrong done to me be upon your head, old man!"

Her flesh was mottled brown by age and the harsh weather. Her hair had grown limp and thin and colorless. Nevertheless, when her body went taut with anger and her eye blazed, Sarai was young again, a warrior.

"The woman whom you embraced," she shouted, "the woman who now has conceived in her Egyptian womb, your maid and my servant—she looks upon me now with contempt," cried Sarai. "I will not abide it, Abram. I will not, and the Lord will have to judge between me and you, therefore!"

Abram stood facing her as she approached. When she paused to draw a breath he said, "She is in your power, Sarai. Do as you please. I won't interfere." Then he returned to his work.

Sarai was left to her own devices. She accepted that as power and freedom, and she became relentless.

From that day forward if Hagar refused to draw water, Sarai commanded two menservants to carry her by the armpits down to the spring and then to carry her back again while she bore the full waterskins however she might. Soon the maid found the strength to go for water on her own.

There were no figs for Hagar now. Nor naps during the day. And Sarai herself cut the Egyptian's hair so close to the skull that the tender skin burned in the sun.

When, finally, Sarai brought the raven-black tresses back to Hagar, together with a stiff linen cap, and required the maid to make of her own long hair a wig; when Sarai announced that she herself would wear the wig on special occasions in company with her husband Abram, Hagar the Egyptian disappeared.

In spite of her condition she ran far away from the tents of Abram—almost to the border of her homeland, Egypt. It was several months before she returned, exhausted, gaunt, but pregnant still.

She told Abram that the angel of the Lord had appeared to her by a spring of water on the way to Shur. The angel had promised her a son: Name him Ishmael, the angel said, for the Lord has heard your affliction. He shall become a wild ass of a man, yet from him shall come so many descendants that they cannot be numbered for multitude.

So Hagar bore Abram a son. And he named the baby Ishmael.

But it was not born on Sarai's knees.

Sarai was forced to watch all these things from a distance.

Yet even at a distance she saw the look on her husband's face as he laid the babe in the crook of his arm: tenderness! The old man's eyes were dewy.

3

Then the Lord appeared to Abram and said, I am El Shaddai. I am God Almighty. Walk before me. Serve me perfectly.

Immediately, Abram fell on his face.

God said to him, Behold, my covenant is with you. No longer shall your name be Abram. You are Abraham, for I have made you the father of a multitude of nations, and I will likewise establish my covenant with your descendants after you—an everlasting covenant!

I give you and your descendants all the land of Canaan—an everlasting possession!

You, Abraham, and every male among you shall be circumcised in the flesh of your foreskins. It shall be a sign of the covenant between me and you.

As for your wife, Sarai: her name shall be Sarah. I will bless her. I will give you a son by her, and kings and peoples shall come from Sarah.

Abraham said, "Shall Sarah bear a child? Oh, that Ishmael might live in your sight, O Lord!"

God said, No! Sarah your wife shall bear you a son and I will establish my covenant with him as an everlasting covenant!

When he had finished saying these things, God went up from Abraham.

Then Abraham took Ishmael his son and all his slaves, every male in his household, and circumcised the flesh of their foreskins that very day, as God had said to him.

4

Although Mamre, where Abraham often encamped, was on ground high enough to grow cool in the evening, during a summer's day the heat of the sun could be intolerable. It was Abraham's habit, then, to raise three sides of his tent on poles in order to cast a shade all round his room and to allow the dry wind to blow through it. Here he would rest in the afternoon, leaning against a straw mat that had been rolled up for his back.

By now the man was ninety-nine years old. He spent the hottest hours of the day dozing. Sometimes his old eye would roll open and he'd watch the oak trees floating in the heat waves; sometimes his eye would close and he would dream; sometimes he'd reach for a waterskin sweating and cooling in the wind.

And so it happened one afternoon that, opening a lazy eye, Abraham saw not trees but people standing by the tent, three men staring down at him. Strangers!

The old man jumped up and bowed down to the ground and said, "Stay a while. Rest a while."

Strangers must also be guests. Therefore, Abraham said, "Sirs, let a little water be brought to wash your feet while I fetch some food for you."

The men said, "Thank you. Do as you have said."

So Abraham went round to Sarah's side of the tent and asked her to make flat cakes of barley meal. He himself ran down to the herds and selected a tender calf for cooking. He roused his household from their afternoon naps and caused a general commotion throughout the encampment.

Finally he returned to his guests and spread goatskins underneath an oak tree and laid out cakes and meat and curds and milk, a generous meal.

He stood to the side and watched while they ate.

When they had finished they said, "Where is your wife? Where is Sarah?"

How could strangers know her name? Her new name! "In the tent," he said.

One of the men dipped his fingers in water to wash them, then leaned against the oak and said, "When I return this way in the spring, your wife Sarah shall be suckling a son."

Abraham felt the hairs on his neck begin to tingle. Suddenly this was not mere dinner conversation. It felt intimate and dangerous.

He was about to respond, when the stranger turned toward the tent and called out, "Sarah! Sarah, why did you laugh?"

A tiny voice in the dark interior said, "I didn't laugh."

The stranger said, "Yes, you did. When I said you would bear a son you laughed in your heart and mumbled, Shall old age have pleasure anymore? Woman," said the stranger, "is anything too hard for the Lord?"

Abraham gaped. His heart had begun to race wildly. His mind could scarcely keep pace with events. The Lord! This fellow had said, Is anything too hard for the Lord?

Once more, louder now but hidden still behind the reed screen of the tent, Sarah said, "I did not laugh!"

The three men were rising up, preparing to travel on. "You did, you know," the more glorious one said. "You laughed."

And then they left. They set out on the long road that descended to the city of Sodom.

For more reasons than he could contemplate, Abraham followed. It was the hospitable thing, surely, to accompany one's guest on his way. But Abraham had recognized in one figure something grander than a guest. By the cold in his bones he suspected that holiness was here. Therefore, Abraham followed, speechless, yet incapable of turning around and going home again.

As dusk darkened the earth, two of the strangers continued down the road alone. The exalted one paused and Abraham, too, stopped.

Then this one spoke in tones transcendent and powerful. It was indeed the Lord who said to Abraham, "The outcry against Sodom and Gomorrah is great. Their sin is very grave. I want to judge whether the accusation is accurate. That is why I am passing this way. That is why I am here."

Abraham glanced south-southwest to the cities in the valley far below. Citizens were lighting the night fires. A hundred tiny fires— they looked like a rash on the earth. Lot lived there.

Abraham closed his eyes and set his jaw. He thought that he should consider carefully his next action, but he could not. He couldn't think at all. He acted.

He said, "Will you destroy the righteous with the wicked?"

The holy figure did not respond.

Abraham wiped his mouth and spoke again. "Suppose there are fifty righteous in the city. Will you spare it for fifty? Surely the judge of all the earth would not slay righteous people because of the wickedness of others."

The Lord said, "If I find fifty righteous in Sodom, I will for their sake spare the city. Yes."

Old Abraham bowed his head and shut his eyes and took a deep breath and spoke. "I know I am but dust and ashes," he said. "But I started to speak and I must finish." He raised his face. "What if there are five less than fifty righteous? Would you destroy the city for lack of five?"

The Lord said, "For forty-five I will spare all."

Abraham said, "Ah, Lord, suppose there are only forty?"

"For forty I will not destroy the city.

"Thirty?"

"If I find thirty righteous I will withhold the punishment."

"What if there are only twenty?"

"And for twenty," said the Lord, "I will spare Sodom."

Abraham discovered that he was breathless, trembling and sweating. But he was not yet finished. "Oh, let not the Lord be angry with me," he said. "I will speak but this once more. Suppose, O Lord, that there are found only ten righteous within the city? What then?"

The Lord said, "For the sake of ten I will not destroy it."

Then the Lord went his way. But Abraham held ground where the dreadful conversation had taken place. He stared down toward Sodom, watching over his nephew Lot. Watching.

Late that same evening two travelers arrived in Sodom. Lot, who was as hospitable as his uncle Abraham, invited them in and fed them and gave them pallets upon which to sleep.

But soon the men of the city surrounded his house, bellowing: "Bring out your visitors that we may lie with them!"

Lot himself stepped out and shut the door. "I beg you, brothers," he said, "don't act so wickedly. These men are my guests. But I have two daughters who are still virgins—"

The men of Sodom only roared the louder, "Get out of the way, Hebrew!" They rushed forward to break down the door.

But immediately the guests, angels of the Lord, snatched Lot in, shut the door, and by a mystery struck blind the entire company of men outside.

The angels said, "The sin of this city is so grievous that the Lord has sent us to destroy it. If there are any people here that you love," they said, "go now and warn them."

In fact, Lot's daughters were betrothed to men whom he respected. He ran to tell them of the Lord's decision. But they laughed outright at his news and scorned any suggestions he made about escaping. Lot was grieved by the prospect of their destruction.

By dawn, then, the angels actually had to drag him, his wife, and his daughters from their house. They drove them through the city gate, saying, "Run for your lives! Don't look back, don't stop in the valley, run to the hills or you will be consumed! Run!"

In the morning Abraham stood on a high hill and watched as fire and pitch and a smoking brimstone rained down upon the cities of Sodom and Gomorrah. Abraham saw heaven lick the valley black, consuming every breathing thing and every green thing that had ever lived there.

When finally smoke went up from Sodom like the smoke of a furnace, the old man sat down and covered his face and wept. "Not even ten!" he said. "O Lot, God could not find as few as ten righteous people in the city you chose for yourself. Where are you now? Where are your daughters? Where is your wife?"

Lot and his daughters were safe in caves. But while they were fleeing the fire, his wife had stopped for a last glance at the city and in that instant had turned into a standing pillar of salt.

5

Soon after the destruction of Sodom, Abraham struck camp and traveled south into the Negev. Near Gerar he found new pasture for his flocks, so he stayed a while.

In the fall he and his men sheared the sheep, causing a daylong bawling from the terrified creatures while the women washed the fleeces clean of dirt and oils. They combed the wool out and packed it in bales. During the winter Abraham's household transported it to the city of Gerar and bartered for articles of copper and bronze, tools, utensils, weapons, pottery—and perhaps something pretty for one's wife if she were about to have a baby.

In the spring the sheep dropped new lambs.

And then the Lord kept his promise to Sarah.

In the small cool hours of a morning, Sarah bore Abraham a boy. The midwife brought the infant outside—a wiry, watchful child—and Abraham could not speak. The old man took the baby and gazed upon skin as fresh as petals—but he could not utter a word.

Eight days later, Abraham circumcised his son with a sharp flint knife. Then he made a great feast, gathering together his whole household to eat and drink and celebrate with him.

And before the day was over, Sarah's joy grew too great to be contained. The old woman laughed. She covered her face and laughed soundlessly, so that the entire company fell silent thinking she was crying. But then she rose up and clapped her hands and sang: "God has made laughter for me! Oh, laugh with me! Let everyone who hears my story laugh! Sisters, sisters, where was your faith? Who guessed yesterday that Sarah would suckle a child today? Yet I have borne my husband an heir in his old age."

Abraham stood to the side watching his wife. Now he went to her and took one of her hands in his own and held it until she stood still and returned his gaze. They were a small, wiry pair beneath the blue firmament.

Then Abraham looked down at Sarah's hand, this cluster of tendons and bone. One by one he touched the brown spots on the back of it. "Old woman, old woman, more precious than rubies," he murmured, "we will name the child for laughter. We will call him Isaac."

She was ninety years old. He was one hundred.

6

At the birth of Ishmael years ago, Abraham had given Hagar her own tent in which to train and raise the boy. Hagar's tent never had pride of place. It was always pitched some distance from Abraham and Sarah's. And through the years Hagar, too, chose to keep distance between herself and the mistress of the household.

Abraham observed the choice and understood.

But privately he watched Ishmael grow into a youth of a nearly animal independence and dark intensities. Though he never spoke the thought aloud, it pleased Abraham to see the lad's spirit emerge both free and eager. On the other hand, it troubled him that the same spirit was wearing Hagar down. Large hands, large feet, her body was rawboned still; but her heart was tired and her mind uncertain.

It was just after Isaac had been weaned and Sarah's breasts were again flat and forever dry, that she came to Abraham among the flocks.

"Cast out," Sarah cried as she approached him, "cast out that slave and her son!"

Abraham turned to face his wife.

She didn't wait for response, but kept talking and coming at once. "I saw that Egyptian's wild whelp playing with little Isaac. There was absolutely no reverence there. None! I saw the future, Abraham, and I won't have it! The son of that slave woman shall not be heir with my son Isaac!"

Abraham said, "He is my son, too."

Sarah stood dead still, staring at Abraham. A little wind tugged at her colorless hair. Her voice, when she spoke, took on a husky quality. She uttered her words with individual softness and care. "Which of these sons," she said, "did the Lord God promise? And which did the Lord God give?"

So Abraham rose early the following morning and carried bread and a skin of water down to Hagar's tent. He spoke a word to her, then put his few provisions on her shoulder and sent her away with the child.

So Hagar and Ishmael went wandering in the wilderness.

But Isaac grew into a comely youth, a son of genuine respect and obedience, the blessing upon his father's old age. Abraham gave his heart completely to the boy.

There were days when the man would take Isaac with him to a high promontory and show him not only the tents, the servants, the flocks and herds of his household, but also the land as far as the lad could see, north and south, east and west.

"I, when I die," Abraham would say, "will give you the tents, my son. But God will give you the land."

The old man loved his son so deeply that he was like life inside his bones.

But then God said, Abraham.

The man said, "Here I am."

And God said, Take your son Isaac to a mount in Moriah and offer him there as a burnt offering to me.

In the evening Abraham carried his straw mat to a private place and unrolled it on a hill. All night he lay gazing up at the stars.

Early in the morning he returned to the tents and cut wood. He saddled a donkey. He asked two servants to accompany him on a journey he was about to make, then he entered Sarah's side of the tent and touched his son to waken him.

"Come," he whispered. "Don't disturb your mother. Come."

So they left the encampment together.

They traveled for three days in a northerly direction.

On the third day the old man lifted his eyes and saw the place of sacrifice afar off.

He said to the servants, "Wait here. The boy and I will go ahead and worship the Lord and then come back to you."

Abraham took the wood and laid it on the back of his son. In his left hand the man bore fire. In his right, the knife. So they walked together toward Moriah.

Isaac said, "Father?"

Abraham said, "Here I am, my son."

Isaac said, "We have the fire and the wood for our sacrifice, but where is the lamb?"

"Ah, the lamb," said Abraham. And then he said, "God will provide." So they continued forward, climbing the side of Moriah together.

When they came to the place, Abraham bent and built an altar. Wiry and silent, the old man laid wood on the altar. Then he bound Isaac his son and lifted him up and laid him on the altar, too, upon the wood.

So then Abraham bound his robe to his waist that nothing hung loosely, and with his left hand he touched the boy at the breastbone, and with his right hand he picked up a long copper knife and raised it very high in order to kill the boy with a single thrust.

Abraham! Abraham! It was the Lord God calling. Abraham!

"Here I am," the old man cried.

God said, Enough. Do not hurt the boy. I know now that you fear God since you did not withhold your only son from me.

Abraham lifted his eyes and saw a ram caught in a thicket by his horns. So he went and took the ram and offered it up as a burnt offering instead of his son. And he called the name of that place The Lord Shall Provide.

And the Lord said, I will indeed bless you. I will multiply your descendants as the stars of heaven, and by them shall all the nations of the earth be blessed—for you have obeyed my voice.

After these things Sarah lived to be a hundred and twenty-seven years old. Abraham was again abiding near the oaks of Mamre. It was there that his old wife died.

Before he spoke the word to anyone else, Abraham sat by her bed for a night and a morning, weeping. He held her hand until it grew cold, and then he laid it by her tiny frame.

At noon he arose and went forth to find a place to bury his dead.

There was a field in Machpelah east of Mamre, owned by a man named Ephron, in which there was a cave. Abraham bartered with Ephron until he agreed to sell his field at a price of four hundred shekels of silver. In the presence of many witnesses the payment was weighed out and the sale made.

So the field belonged to Abraham.

He carried his wife Sarah to his small property and brought her into the cave and buried her there.

REBEKAH

1

Outside the city where Abraham's brother, Nahor, had lived and died, there was a well of fresh spring water. Abundant and dependable, the well served both the town and the travelers who passed by, caravans bearing rich goods east and west.

In order to draw water from this particular well, a woman had to descend steps of uneven stone, kneel down and dip her jar in the flowing water, then heave the full container back up to her shoulder and climb the steps again. Beasts of burden, of course, could not go down in the grotto themselves, so their water was brought up by the jarful and poured into stone troughs built at ground level.

Rebekah was familiar with the well and the routine. Daily at dusk she went with a group of friends to draw water for their families—bright young women, jars on their shoulders and laughter rising like flocks of birds. Rebekah herself moved more quietly than the others. She was tall. She took a longer, more graceful stride. She had a forehead of intelligence and a manner of immediate conviction. Even surrounded by crowds this woman seemed to stand alone.

And so it happened one evening that as the women were coming up from the well with full jars, an old man stepped forward and spoke to Rebekah as if she were the only one around.

"Please," he said, "may I have a drink from your jar?"

Clearly he was a traveler, dusty from the road, tired and very old—old enough to be her grandfather. Rebekah saw ten camels kneeling here and there around the well, their heads on high.

Her friends watched a moment, then left. It was growing dark, and Rebekah could take care of herself.

"Yes," she said, lowering the jar to her hand. "Yes, please do drink."

He took just a sip, never removing his eyes from her face. It caused her to blush.

She said, "I'll draw water for your camels, too, sir."

And she did. Down and up the stone steps she went, pouring water into the drinking troughs. While the old man still gazed at her, she gave a proper thump to one beast, which then rose and ambled forward to drink. The others followed. And Rebekah kept filling the troughs until all ten camels were satisfied.

It was dark when she was done.

And when the old man again approached her, he held in his hand objects so smooth and beautiful that they shined. A golden ring and two gold bracelets.

"Whose daughter are you?" he said.

Rebekah answered, "I am the daughter of Bethuel who is the son of Nahor."

"Nahor," the stranger murmured, "I know Nahor." He said the name with such emotion that he seemed about to burst into tears. He reached for Rebekah's hand and gently slipped the ring onto her finger. "Does Bethuel's house have room for me and my people to lodge a while?"

She said, "We have straw and provender, yes. And room. Yes."

Now, the old man went down on his knees and raised his arms and chanted softly: "Blessed be the Lord, the God of my master Abraham! He has led me to the house of his kinsman."

Without rising again, he clasped the bracelets around Rebekah's arms and said, "Please go. Please beg space for me for the night."

Rebekah's father was old and infirm by then. It was her brother Laban who made most of the family's decisions. Laban didn't take an immediate interest in this story about a traveler from the west. He kept eating his supper. But then Rebekah removed her robe; he saw the gold and straightway left the house.

While he was gone, Rebekah and her mother prepared more food.

In time they heard Laban's voice outside. He was himself unbridling the man's camels. He was commanding his servants to bring water for the man's feet. And then he was saying, "Come in, O blessed of the Lord. Come and eat."

But when they were in the house and food was placed before him, the old man refused to eat.

"Not till I have told my errand," he said.

Laban said, "Speak on, friend!"

So he said, "I am Abraham's servant. The Lord has greatly blessed my master with flocks and herds, with silver and gold, menservants, maidservants, camels, and asses.

"But Abraham has only one son. Isaac. And he made me swear in the land of Canaan to return to this land and to the house of his kindred, here to find a wife for Isaac.

"This very day I arrived at the well outside your city and prayed that God would prosper me in my task. I said, O Lord, when I ask a young woman to give me a drink, if she says, 'Drink, and I will draw for your camels, too,' let her be the woman you've chosen for my master's son.

"And behold, even before I was done praying, your sister came. Rebekah came. This beautiful woman came and did all that I had asked of the Lord.

"Now, then," said the old man to Laban and Bethuel, "if you will deal loyally and honestly with my master, say so. And if not, say that, too. I must know whether to turn to the right hand or the left."

Laban said, "Clearly the thing comes from the Lord. Take my sister and go. Let her be the wife of your master's son, as the Lord has spoken."

All this Rebekah heard in shadow and in silence, standing erect in the same room while the men sat low around the oil lamp, speaking to one another.

It was Abraham's servant who finally raised his eyes and acknowledged her. "Rebekah, daughter of Bethuel," he said. She took several steps into the light, and he said, "Receive these things." Then he handed her jewels of silver and gold, and raiment closely woven. He also gave her brother and her mother costly ornaments.

Finally he ate his supper.

In the morning he said to his hosts, "Please allow me to go back to my master now. He's old and cannot live much longer."

Laban said, "Oh, sir—no! Let the maiden take time to say good-bye. Be our guest in the meantime. At least ten days."

"Please," said the servant. "The journey is a long one. The season will turn to rain soon. Please."

Laban said, "We should let Rebekah decide."

Immediately Rebekah said, "I will go."

Thus did Rebekah, this woman of quick conviction and utter self-assurance, in a night and a day transform her life thereafter and forever.

In the month that followed, Rebekah and the old servant traveled from her home in Paddan-aram on the same road Abraham himself had taken more than sixty-five years earlier, a long southward route. They crossed the Jordan River at Succoth and journeyed yet farther south than the Salt Sea into the Negev.

On the evening of the thirtieth day, while the camels were moving with weary languor, Rebekah lifted her eyes and saw a man strolling alone across the fields, his head bent down in meditation.

"Who is that?" she said.

She alighted from her camel and went to the old servant of Abraham. "Do you see that man in the distance?" she asked. "Who is he?"

"Ah, that's the son of my master. That is Isaac."

So Rebekah covered her face with a veil and waited to be seen by the man who would be her husband.

In the Negev, then, Isaac took Rebekah to his tent, and she became his wife, and he loved her completely. He never loved another as long as he lived.

He said, "As soon as I saw the woman standing tall by the side of a white field, I fell in love with her."

He was forty years old.

2

At the age of a hundred and seventy-five, Abraham breathed his last and died, an old man full of years.

His two sons came to bury him in the cave of Machpelah, in the field which he had purchased as a burial place for his wife.

So they were gathered together in the end, Abraham and Sarah.

But the brothers Isaac and Ishmael went their separate ways, never to meet again.

The children of Ishmael lived in the wilderness of Paran. They became a wild, fighting tribe, their young men expert with the bow, their hands against all other tribes.

But after the death of Abraham, God blessed Isaac.

For the next twenty years he wandered throughout the Negev wilderness, sojourning with his flocks and herds in the lands of other people, living in tents as Abraham had done before him.

And like Sarah before her, Rebekah was barren.

3

"Isaac, why does the king want to see us?"

"Who knows why kings do anything?"

"No, but you know something. There's something you're not telling me."

"Well, yesterday when we were lying in the barley field Abimelech saw us."

"So what? Why should a king care about someone else's loving?" It wasn't so much a question as a meditation. Rebekah was beginning to wonder whether Isaac ought to strike camp and move away from this place— even before the harvest, if necessary.

She was riding a handsome donkey. A light breeze tugged at her veil. Her husband had insisted that she veil herself for this particular interview. Isaac himself was washed and well dressed, leading the donkey up a long road toward the whitewashed walls of the Philistine city called Gerar.

They had been dwelling in this region for several seasons now, maintaining a fairly peaceful accord with the king and his people. In the beginning Isaac had even spent time in the city gates, gossiping with the citizens.

But lately his flocks and fields had been prospering more than those of Gerar. And when his servants discovered a fresh water in an old well, the men of Gerar came and demanded it for themselves. Isaac shrugged and gave it over and ordered his servants to dig another well. But when that well also brought forth a sweet water, the same men came to claim it, this time armed and angry, ready to fight. Isaac didn't want a fight. Though he himself was a good hunter he was not a fighting man. He relinquished this well, too.

So Rebekah was thinking that it was time for them to rise up and travel elsewhere.

Suddenly she snapped out of her meditations. "Isaac," she said sharply, "I think I want you to answer that question."

"What question?"

"Why Abimelech should be concerned about our lying together. If a wife wants children, what is that to a king?"

"A wife," Isaac mumbled low. "A wife, yes. Not a sister."

"What? What did you say?"

"I said, 'Not a sister.'"

"Isaac, turn and look at me! What do you mean, not a sister?"

Isaac turned but did not look at his wife. He said, "When we first came here the men of Gerar saw how beautiful you are, and they asked about you. I was afraid they might kill the husband to get at his wife—but for a sister they would let the brother alone. I told them you were my sister."

Rebekah gazed at Isaac a while, sitting as straight as a rod of iron upon her mount. Then she removed her veil and gathered her robes tightly around her body, snatched the bridle from her husband's hand, turned the donkey and rode alone back to the tents. Let Isaac keep his interview with the king. Let Isaac explain his own folly. Let Isaac grant her respectability again and with a confession make her his wife for the second time.

But now she was convinced. The time had come to move on.

4

As her husband approached the sixtieth year of his life, Rebekah and Isaac encamped again at Beer-lahai-roi, near the same field where they first set eyes on one another.

She was younger than he, but they had been married for twenty years without children, and Rebekah longed for children.

One night she wept loudly and angrily on account of her longing.

The following morning Isaac came into her compartment, took her hand, and led her to a high, rocky hill where he lifted his hands in prayer on his wife's behalf. Then they went back down to their tent. They spent the rest of the day together, and soon Rebekah had no need to cry for want of a child. She had conceived. She was smiling and radiant again, and pregnant.

Ah, dark Rebekah! When she smiled her eye was the secret moon in a black galena sky. Her passage was so slow and so graceful as to bind men's hearts to the vision forever.

At three months to term Rebekah began to experience crushing pains in her womb. She would suddenly cry out, then clap her hand across her mouth in order to cover the sound.

If it has to be this way, she thought, why should I go on living?

This time she went alone to the sacred hill where Isaac had prayed before. She raised her hands and said, "What is it, Lord? O Lord, what is happening to me?"

And the Lord God said:

Two nations are wrestling
 within your womb;
two peoples born of your body,
  Rebekah,
shall suffer a lasting division.

One shall be stronger than the other;
the elder shall serve his younger brother.

And so it was that when the time came for Rebekah to be delivered, she gave birth to twin boys. The first one came out wrinkled and red and so hairy he seemed to be wearing a coat. And the second came immediately behind, clutching his brother's heel.

So they named the first infant Esau. And the next they named Jacob, because already within the womb he was seizing his brother's heel.

5

As he grew into adulthood, Esau became a plainsman. Like his father he would go away by himself for months at a time, living off the land. Hunting. He had an accurate eye and an instinctive knowledge of his quarry: gazelle, oryx, ibex and all wild goats, mountain sheep—beasts of a gamier taste than fattened, domestic animals. A broad-chested, red-haired man, Esau lived by the strength of his arm. Even when he sat among the tents, he was not given to much talk.

Jacob, on the other hand, stayed continually in range of the household, the flocks, and fields and tents. He dearly loved a cunning conversation. Jacob's face, like his mother's, was smooth and mobile with intelligence. And he was a verbal fellow, more confident of his wit than of his arm.

Their father Isaac loved the game Esau brought home and cooked for him.

Their mother loved Jacob.

One wintry dawn Esau returned from a long and unsuccessful hunt. He hadn't eaten for several days, and he had just traveled an entire night afoot. He was starving.

As he approached the tents of his father he smelled a morning stew on the air. It tightened his stomach and made him mad for food. He followed the scent directly to the tent of his brother.

There sat Jacob, stirring a bubbling red pottage.

Esau could scarcely form the words. "Please," he groaned, pointing toward the clay pot. "Please, Jacob, I am dying—"

Jacob said nothing for a moment. Then he looked up and smiled. "I think we can make a bargain," he said.

Esau wiped a big hand across his mouth. "A bargain?"

Jacob grinned and uttered his next words with such swift articulation that Esau felt at first confused, then angry, and then just hungry, careless of anything else.

"Can a dead man inherit his father's wealth," Jacob said, "even if that man happens to be the elder of two brothers only? No, of course not. Dead men inherit nothing at all. If you die, brother, you've got nothing here and can get nothing hereafter. But if I give you food, I give you life now. In return for your life, then, you must give me that which, without your life, can mean nothing at all to you. Your birthright. So then here is the bargain, Esau: I give you life, you give me your birthright, and we are even."

Jacob always talked like this, too fast for common folk to follow. Esau could only think of food. "Yes," he said, reaching for the pot.

But Jacob pulled it back and with eyes suddenly steadfast said, "Swear it to me, Esau."

Esau yelled, "I swear," snatched the pot by main strength and carried it away in order to eat without the noise of his brother's voice to annoy him.

In the days of their youth, most children give more thought to present desires than to the future necessities. Though it may mean nothing to a young man then when his blood is high and his arm is strong and his father is healthy, a birthright is a terrible thing to lose. It is double the inheritance any other sibling will receive.

Rebekah knew that.

More than that, Rebekah knew of the peculiar blessing which had been handed from Abraham to his son, her husband.

For the Lord God had also appeared to Isaac in the night, saying, Fear nothing, Isaac. I am with you. I will bless you and multiply your descendants for the sake of Abraham my servant.

The very next day Isaac built an altar in that place, and worshiped the God of his father. Rebekah had watched the mystery of her husband's behavior, and she had learned thereby both the faith and the prosperity of the family into which she had married.

6

When Isaac had grown old and blind, he called Esau into his compartment and said, "I do not know the day of my death, except that it shall be soon. Now, then, Esau, take your bow and hunt game for me and prepare the savory food I love, that I may eat and bless you before I die."

As soon as Esau left the tents for the fields, Rebekah called Jacob into her compartment and whispered, "Don't talk, just listen. Just now your father sent Esau out to kill and cook meat for a very important meal. He plans to bless your brother before the Lord." Rebekah took Jacob's face between her hands and gazed sharply into his eyes. "There is no other blessing like the one he is about to bestow upon your brother," she said. "It is the blessing his father gave to him, the blessing of God which promises children and land to him who is blessed with it!

"Therefore, go down to the goat herd and slaughter two kids. I will cook one the way your father likes it, savory, and you will carry the meat to him so that he blesses you first."

Jacob whispered, "But Esau is hairy and I'm smooth. My father will feel the difference."

"What's hairier than a goat?" Rebekah said. "That's why you will kill two kids, one for its pelt. We'll cover your neck and arms with a good thick fur."

"But what if my father discovers me? What if I get a curse instead of a blessing?"

"Keep your voice down," said his mother. Then she hugged him briefly and said, "Upon me shall be the curse, my son. As for you, obey my word!"

So Jacob ran out and slaughtered two small goats with his own hand. Rebekah began to cook the one while Jacob skinned the other and scraped fat from the inside of the hide with the long edge of a knife. This fresh fur they tied to the backs of his hands, to his neck and shoulders—and over that they pulled one of the robes Esau used when hunting.

Rebekah placed a savory broiled meat into Jacob's hand and whispered, "Go."

So he entered his father's compartment bearing food.

"My father," said Jacob.

Isaac, sitting low upon his pallet, said, "Here I am. Who are you, son?"

Jacob said, "I am Esau. Your firstborn. I have done what you asked. Please sit up and eat that you might bless me—"

Isaac turned his blind face to the side. "Already?" he said. "How did you find game so quickly?"

"God gave me the speed."

Isaac said, "Come here, son. Let me touch you."

So Jacob drew near unto him, and Isaac stroked the goat hair. "The skin is Esau's," he murmured, "but the voice is Jacob's. Are you truly Esau?"

Jacob said, "Yes. I am."

Isaac said, "Let me kiss you."

Jacob bent down and held very still while his father kissed his neck at the hem of the hunting robe.

Finally Isaac said, "Yes. It smells like Esau, yes. So let me eat of your game, my son, and I will bless you."

When he had eaten, the old man spread his hands over the young man and, rocking to the rhythm of his language, chanted:

> *I smell the soil,*
>> *I smell the field the Lord has blessed!*
> *May Heaven likewise*
>> *grant you fatness, grains and grapes,*
>>> *both bread and wine abundantly.*
> *May peoples serve you,*
>> *your mother's sons bow down before you!*
> *If any curse you*
>> *he will be cursed,*
>>> *and blessed be all who bless you, son,*
>>>> *forevermore.*

And so it was done. Old Isaac subsided into weariness, and Jacob left the tent.

Almost immediately Esau returned from the hunt with a fine catch. He dressed and cooked the meat and brought it into Isaac's compartment.

"Father," he said, "arise, eat the meat you love so much, then bless me as you said."

"Eat?" said Isaac, raising his head, blinking rapidly. "Eat? And what do you mean, 'Bless you'? Who is this? Who are you?"

"I am your son," said Esau. "I am your firstborn son—"

"Esau?" Isaac widened his blind eyes.

"Yes, Esau. And I have obeyed your word—"

"Then who was here before you?" Isaac cried. "Whose food have I eaten—"

"What?" Esau whispered.

"—and who did I bless—"

"Father! What are you saying?"

"—yes, and he shall be blessed—"

"You blessed someone instead of me? O Father!"

Esau lifted his voice in a wild, bitter cry: "Father, Father, Father," he wailed, "bless me also, O my father!"

Isaac said miserably, "Your brother has taken away your blessing, Esau."

"Jacob!" cried Esau. "Oh, they were right to name you Jacob! Twice have you tripped me from my rightful place."

"And I," whispered Isaac, "I have given him lordship over you."

Esau fell down to his knees and wept, "O Father, is there nothing left for me? Not one blessing left?"

The old man grew quiet. Finally he raised his hands above his elder son and spoke softly:

> *Far from fatness shall you live,*
> *far from grain and grapes and wine;*
> *and by the sword you must survive,*
> *serving Jacob for a time.*
>
> *But when you break the yoke of your brother,*
> *it shall be broken, my son, forever!*

So the second blessing, lesser than the first, was given.

And so Esau went forth from the tent of Isaac breathing threats against his younger brother: "I'll wait until our father dies," he said. "But then I will kill Jacob."

In the early dark hours of the following morning, Rebekah slipped into Jacob's tent and woke him. "Get up," she whispered, stroking his cheek and chin. "Jacob, get up. Your brother has taken an oath to murder you. Flee to my family in the old country, Haran. Run to your uncle Laban. When Esau's anger has cooled, I will call you home again. But for now, go. Why should I lose two sons in a single day?"

So then Rebekah stood on a high rocky hill and watched the shadow of her dear one go. Softly he stole away as dawn began to touch the eastern sky.

Rebekah never sent the message that Jacob could come home again. She died before she believed in his safety. She died without seeing her son again, and she was gathered to her husband's people, to Abraham and Sarah in the cave of Machpelah.

JACOB

1

Jacob ran a ridge road north by northeast. He kept to the spine of the hills which rose toward the oaks at Mamre, where his grandfather had so often sojourned. A stony road, it tore his sandals and cut his feet, but it didn't hit high bluffs or drop into impassable gorges. He felt the breath of his brother's threats upon his back. Jacob was outrunning his own death.

At noon he rested beneath an acacia tree—but grew too anxious to be still and then ran the rest of the afternoon without another pause. By evening the sun was low on his left, casting into darkness the treacherous descent toward the Salt Sea on his right.

Even into the night Jacob kept running, now tasting blood in his mouth, breathing hoarsely.

Then—in a barren place, suddenly—his legs failed him. He pitched face forward to the ground and lay still. He smelled the soil and the rock beneath his cheek. Above him the multitude of stars, the hosts of heaven, filled blackness with such tiny lights that the man felt diminished and solitary. His throat was raw. His muscles had seized like iron bands within him. The ground was cold. But he did not move. His head lay on a smooth rock. So then: that smooth rock would be his pillow. Jacob fell asleep.

And while he slept, he dreamed.

In his dream the night sky was completely empty, black, bereft of stars; but yet there was a falling and rising brightness near him. He looked and saw a broad staircase set with its foot on the earth and its head as high as the doors of heaven, and the angels of God were ascending and descending the staircase, coming and going, performing the myriad purposes of God.

He looked again, and there—standing above all, above the endless flight of stairs and the angels and the earth—he saw the Lord God himself.

And the Lord spoke to Jacob.

He said, I am the Lord, the God of Abraham and the God of Isaac. The land whereon you lie I will give to you and to your descendants. And your descendants shall be like the dust for multitude. And in you shall all the nations of the earth be blessed.

Behold, said the Lord, I am with you. I will keep you wherever you wander. And I will bring you back to this land. I will never leave you, never, until I have kept my promises—

Suddenly Jacob awoke from his dream, shaking with fear.

The night was visible again. The tiny stars had returned to their places, cold and distant. But nothing was the same. An acrid scent of the sacred lingered near the earth.

"Surely," Jacob whispered, "the Lord is in this place, and I did not know it!" He rose to his knees. "Why, this is none other than the house of God! And this," he said, gazing upward, "is the gate of heaven."

Even as the sunrise began to enflame the eastern sky, Jacob took hold of his pillow-rock and heaved it from the ground. He set it on end as a pillar and poured oil over it to mark the holiness of the place.

"O Lord," he cried, "if you will keep me and if you will bring me again to my father's house in peace, then you shall be my God—and this standing stone shall be your house."

So he named the place Beth-El, The House of God. And he went on his journey less lonely after that.

2

When Abraham had traveled this route a hundred years ago, he came with flocks and herds and a sizable household. The days of his journey were at least three times the days of Jacob's. Even Abraham's servant, when he rode ten camels back to Haran to find a wife for Isaac, took longer than Isaac's son did.

Jacob was light on his feet, young and healthy and swift after all.

After twenty days he came into a wide, flat plain where one could see great distances unobstructed. There were sheep there. Jacob saw three flocks of sheep, all lying down at noonday—not grazing abroad, as he himself would have chosen if they had been his flocks.

Then he saw the shepherds. They, too, were lying down, their hands behind their heads. Beside them, unremoved, was a heavy stone upon the mouth of a cistern of water. So, then: not only were the flocks not grazing; neither were they drinking, though the water was there for them.

"My brothers!" Jacob called as he approached the shepherds. They turned their eyes toward him, but no one rose to greet him.

"Where am I?" he asked. "Where do you come from?"

A lean man said, "Haran."

"Haran? Truly?" Jacob grinned. He could scarcely believe his good fortune. "Where? Which way to Haran?"

The same man pointed north. Jacob looked and saw a fourth flock coming slowly through the sunlight.

"Is it possible that you know Laban?" he asked. "Does anyone know Laban, the son of Bethuel?"

Another man nodded. "We know him."

"Then I'm here!" cried Jacob. "This is exactly where I'm supposed to be." Several shepherds cast wry glances at the young man. Jacob said, "How is Laban? Is it well with him?"

The same lean shepherd said, "Yes, of course. Why not? That one has sons and daughters enough to care for his stock. Look there. That's one of his daughters coming now. Rachel."

"Rachel," Jacob said softly, glancing at the figure coming in her blowing robes.

Then with more vigor he said, "Why is everyone lying around? It's noon. Why don't you water your flocks and lead them off to pasture?"

Now, the lean shepherd squinted at Jacob as if to take his first true look at this foreigner, then turned over on his stomach. "It's the rule," he said. "No one waters his flock from this cistern till all the flocks are here. Besides, it takes more than three men to move the stone."

Rachel. As she came closer ahead of her flock, Jacob couldn't help but stare at her. Rachel: her eyes were wide and shy, as moist as the eyes of a ewe lamb, and as kind. She had a beautiful fall of dark hair. She was herself small, her bones delicate, but she moved with such an economy that she seemed strong withal.

Moreover, she didn't have to utter a word. All she did was glance in Jacob's direction, and immediately the young man leaped to serve her. By himself he hooked his hands beneath the cistern stone, lifted it, and rolled it aside. He rushed to her, took the jar she was carrying, and began with speed and splashing to descend and ascend the steps of the cistern, pouring water down troughs for the sake of her flock alone.

The shepherds who had so little energy before now came running with their own flocks and jars and cursings. Who did this fellow think he was, breaking the rules?

But this fellow had lost all interest in brother shepherds. His eyes were filled with this sister shepherd who stood quietly by and waited till her sheep were satisfied. Then she smiled and, in tones as musical as the turtledove's, said, "Thank you, sir."

The very sound of her voice released such a rush of lonely emotion that Jacob walked toward her with tears in his eyes.

"Rachel, daughter of Laban," he whispered, "I am Jacob. I am the son of your father's sister, Rebekah."

"Jacob?" she said. "My father's kinsman, Jacob?"

He nodded and smiled and kissed her. "Jacob."

So Rachel ran north to Haran. And soon Laban himself came running back across the plain, a short, round, balding man, breathless from the run but full of compliments and attentions for his nephew. He threw his arms around Jacob and kissed him and led him by the elbow all the way back to his house.

"My bone and my flesh!" he announced. "You must stay with me at least a month."

During that month Jacob worked for his uncle Laban with eagerness and a tireless efficiency. I will be no lazy shepherd, he thought. I'll make myself indispensable.

Therefore, he learned the lay of the land around Haran, the places of best pasturage, the caves where he might, if necessary, protect sheep from wild beasts or bad weather, the springs and wells and cisterns scattered in the wilderness. No matter where the shepherd led his flock, it must always be within a day's reach of water.

Laban's family lived in round stone houses with roofs of flat stone laid on wooden beams which radiated from a central pillar. The roofs were plastered and did not leak. Until this month Jacob had always dwelt in tents.

Moreover, Laban had created an elaborate system of sheepfolds by means of many low, stone walls. All his flocks could therefore return in the same night and still be kept separate.

In the evenings Jacob watched as hundreds of sheep and goats came home. He had a quick eye for the slightest limp and an easy hand with the crook to single out the sick kid. Better yet, he knew how to bind a wound and heal an infection.

At the end of a month Laban came to Jacob rubbing his jaw and shaking his head.

"Son of my sister," he said, slapping the young man's back, "I don't think I can do without you anymore. I have sons of my own, of course. And daughters, as you know very well: Leah, the older, and Rachel, the younger. Excellent children, all of them. Good workers, too. But you! You—" He started to laugh. Jacob, too, laughed. They laughed together.

"Will you stay?" said Laban. "Will you work for me? I'll pay you, nephew. You name your wage and we have a deal."

Jacob knew exactly the wage that he wanted.

"Rachel," he said.

Laban's smile stuck. "What? Who?"

Jacob said, "Sir, I'll serve you seven years for your younger daughter, Rachel." His grin, when he pronounced the name, was dazzling; but his eye had a naked quality and a flash of panic: "That she might be my wife," he said.

Laban said, "Better I give the girl to you than to any other man. We have a deal."

For seven years Jacob went forth every morning singing.

Everyone in Laban's house knew when Jacob was putting on his leather sandals and his cloak of leather. He sang about them. He sang about the girdle he wore. He named each bit of food in his scrip: bread, cheese, dates, raisins. To him his water bag contained a wine of criminal sweetness. And curdled goat's milk was the meat of kings and queens.

So he strode forth ahead of his flocks carrying three weapons: a sling, a stout studded club, and a voice of such garrulous confidence that any wild beast who heard him coming fled.

"Such long black lashes on these ewe lambs!" he sighed. "Eyes like Rachel's eyes."

He would lie on the ground in the midst of the flock, murmuring, "I'm surrounded by a host of Rachels!"

And the time passed as easily as a river at high water. Jacob the son of Isaac was very happy.

At the end of seven years, Jacob washed himself, perfumed his hair, put on fresh clothes and new sandals, and went to the house of his uncle Laban.

"Sir," he said, "it's time. The years of my service are complete, and I wish now to marry your daughter."

Laban said, "Yes, it is surely time that you marry a daughter of mine!"

So the father of the bride sent out invitations to all the people of that region.

On the wedding day women gathered with Laban's wife and daughters in their private rooms to prepare the bride. By afternoon men had crowded into Laban's court-yards where they ate and enjoyed a variety of entertain-ments. Jacob sat in a seat of high dignity, beaming, speechless.

Finally at midnight Laban escorted his daughter, veiled face and foot in the most expensive raiment, to Jacob the bridegroom; then he led the couple through a pathway of grinning guests to a newly-built house, the doorway of which was graced by a carved stone lintel.

To the groom he said, "Here is your wife for the rest of your life. Take pleasure in her, my son."

The bride he admonished with these words: "My daughter, hold your tongue. Obey your husband ever in a humble silence."

Then he cried, "Tonight, no lights! Pleasure only, my dear children!" And he shut the door upon them.

In time the wedding guests departed, both the men and the women. Servants cleared away all signs of cele-bration.

In the morning there rose from Jacob's new house such a roaring that half of Haran woke.

Jacob burst out and crossed the courtyard to Laban's door. He didn't knock. He went straight inside and pointed at the man on his pallet, shouting, "What have you done to me?"

Jacob struck his forehead with a fist. "I served you for Rachel," he cried. "It is Rachel I love. All night long

I thought I was with Rachel. Rachel! But this morning I look, and what do I see? I see Leah! Leah of the weak eyes! Leah! Why have you deceived me, old man?"

Laban sat up with a wounded look on his face. "How can you say such things to me?" he said. "One would think you were an enemy, not a nephew."

"Enemy?" shrieked Jacob. "Fraud! You are a fraud and not a father!"

"Please, Jacob. Please, let's not argue so," said Laban, smooth as honey. "Harsh words hurt me. This is all a mere misunderstanding."

He stood and reached up to pat Jacob's shoulder. "We have a custom here. I thought you knew. In this country we let the firstborn marry first, and the second-born second. It's the natural sequence. But," said Laban, throwing open his arms to embrace his son-in-law, "if you will serve me another seven years, you may marry the second-born, too. Within the week, in fact! Within the week you may lead the lovely Rachel, too, to your new stone house." The short man stood back and smiled. "What do you say? Do we have a bargain?"

Jacob's face was black as thunder. But his voice was small muttering, and he said, "Yes."

"What? What did you say, nephew?"

"Yes," said Jacob. "We have a bargain."

3

Leah Speaks:

When my husband discovered that I was not my sister, I did not blame him for his anger. I had expected anger. I only hoped he would not hit me, and he didn't. He scarcely looked at me. At me, I mean. He did not see Leah. He saw not-Rachel.

Mine was the more elaborate wedding, of course, being first. Louder. More food, more guests.

It was when he led my sister into the same room where one week earlier he had led me; it was when he asked me to leave my new house and return to my mother's house a while; it was when he went into my sister fully knowing who she was and able, therefore, to call her by name; it was then that I surprised myself with sorrow.

I had said I would not love him. But I failed.

Thereafter I cooked well, and he praised my food. But he lingered over Rachel's.

At shearing time he weighed our portions of wool evenly. Each bundle was the balance of the other. But Rachel's wool, when it was washed, showed not a fiber that was not white.

I tried to hide my sorrow. It had not been planned that I should love Jacob. Nor was it his fault that I did. So he did not see my heart. But the Lord saw.

The Lord soon opened my womb and I conceived and I carried the baby nine months and I bore for my husband his firstborn son. I named him Reuben, because the Lord had looked upon my affliction, and I thought: Surely now my husband, too, will notice me.

Not long after that I conceived again and bore another son, and I thought, Because the Lord has heard that I am hated, he has given me this son also. So I named him Simeon.

Again I conceived and bore a son and I called him Levi. I thought that surely now my husband would be joined to me, seeing that I had borne him three sons.

Well, but I who was rich in one thing was poor in the other. Jacob loved his children, yes. And since that first night he nevermore looked with anger at me. Simply, he did not look at me with anything at all, neither a thought nor a word nor a feeling. When he looked at me he did not see Leah. He saw not-Rachel.

While I was bearing children all those years, my sister was barren. She was unhappy. So Jacob was unhappy, too.

I heard them whispering at midnight.

She said, "Jacob, either you give me children like Leah, or I shall die!"

He said, "Ah, Rachel, do you think I am in the place of God? I'm not the one who closed your womb."

When, therefore, I conceived and bore another son, I no longer sought the love of my husband by means of my children. I said out loud, "This time I will praise the Lord!" And I named the baby Judah.

But this fourth child tormented my sister. She stopped talking to me. She ignored my four sons. And if ever she was saying something to Jacob when I drew near, she broke it off and glared at me.

I saw that Jacob's shoulders began to droop and his eyes grew tired.

Then I saw that Rachel's maid, Bilhah, was with child, and I understood. Bilhah bore the baby upon my sister's knees, so it was considered to be Rachel's; and as soon as she saw that it was a boy she cried, "God has judged me and has heard my voice and has given me a son!" She named him Dan to commemorate this judgment of God.

Within a year Rachel's maid bore another son. I was not in the room at the time, yet the whole family heard Rachel's voice ring out when the boy was born. She said: "With mighty wrestlings have I wrestled with my sister, and I have prevailed." The word she used for "wrestle" is niphtal. So she named the baby Naphtali.

Shall I be blamed for offering my husband my maid then, too? By Zilpah I had two more sons. I named the first one Gad because he was for me good fortune; and the second I named Asher: Happy. And why should I not be happy, seeing that I was now the mother of six?

Still, my sister was not happy.

One morning during the wheat harvest my oldest son found mandrake roots. Roots shaped like a little man. They help women to bear boys. Rachel must have noticed. That afternoon she came to the threshing floor where I was working, picked up a flail, and began to beat the wheat beside me. Then she astonished me by speaking.

"Give me some of Reuben's mandrake," she said.

Those are the first words my sister had spoken to me in more than ten years. God forgive me, mine were no kinder than hers.

"Why should I?" I said. "Does the woman who stole my husband's love now want my son's roots, too?"

"Jacob visits you," she said.

"Not for years, Rachel," I said. "With Zilpah, yes. Not with me."

"Not for a single night?"

"Well, you tell me which night he has not been with you, and that will be the night he spent with me."

"Not one?"

"None."

Rachel fell silent, swinging her double stick, thumping the hard dirt, beating the wheat-sheaves into kernel and chaff—while I said nothing. I had covered my face with my skirt. I did not want my sister to see that I was crying.

But then she stopped threshing and I felt her hand on the back of my neck.

"Leah," she said, "let's make a trade. I'll give you nights with Jacob, this night now and others hereafter, and we will not be enemies anymore, but sisters. And will my sister then give me some of her son's mandrake roots?"

This is the moment in my story which I most want to tell: that I embraced my sister. We burst into tears and held one another, and I found how deeply I loved her. No, I had never ceased to love the beautiful Rachel.

The mandrake did not help her. But she helped me. I bore two more sons and a daughter after that, and for each birth my sister was my midwife. We named the first of these three Issachar, and the second Zebulun, and the little girl Dinah. That was the end of my childbearing. I gave birth to no more children.

But my sister did.

Finally God hearkened to our ceaseless prayer on her behalf and opened her womb and the entire family rejoiced when Rachel conceived and bore a son.

On that day Jacob remembered how to smile again. Ah, his face was a flood of sunlight. He was happy. I was happy.

And Rachel gave beautiful voice to her own happiness. She said, "The Lord God has taken my reproach away!"

She named her first son Joseph.

4

When Laban was happy he would grin so hard, that he produced beads of sweat on the top of his bald head. Lately the short man was sweating all the time, always dandling some new grandchild on his knee.

Jacob, the son of his sister Rebekah, had been for him an incalculable treasure. Ever since the young man's arrival nineteen years ago, Laban's flocks had continued to redouble themselves. Moreover, because his nephew held the rank of a servant in the household, the laws of the land gave Laban authority over Jacob's wives—his daughters—and over all their children.

Laban couldn't say that he'd actually planned such a rich old age; but neither would he deny that he deserved it. It was his cunning that had caused it, after all; a lesser man would not now be sitting so easy, dandling grandsons.

But there came a morning when Laban stepped outside to find Jacob standing by the door, hunched, haggard, and brooding.

"My son, what's the matter?" Laban boomed, full of good will.

Jacob said, "I have to leave Haran."

"What did you say?"

Jacob looked directly at Laban. "Sir, I beg you to let me go."

"Go? So you're speaking of going somewhere. Where?"

"Home."

"Ah," said Laban. "Of course. A visit."

"No, sir. No," said Jacob. He wore a full beard now, grizzled grey with his working. He was broad-shouldered; no day went by when he did not bend his back to some heavy labor. But he had in these latter years descended into silence. Who knew why talkative young men gave up that grander part of themselves? Laban, on the other hand, had kept his tongue oiled and was proud of his ready speech.

"Say on, my son," he said.

Jacob drew a deep breath. "You yourself know how your herds have increased all the years I've served you," he said. "And you know how honest I've been. Please, sir: release your daughters to me. Let me take my children and return to the land of my fathers. I want to be wandering again. This sitting in one place—" Jacob shook his head. "This working all in one place for so long . . . I . . . Laban, I haven't even been able to lay anything by for my family!"

"Right!" cried Laban. He seized Jacob's arm. "Exactly right! You must provide for your family before you do anything else! Before you even think of leaving, we must negotiate some better wage for you and the children. Tell me what you want, and it is yours."

Jacob gazed at his uncle a moment. He turned and looked toward the sheepfolds, then back at his uncle again. "Nothing," he said. "I don't want you to give me anything—"

"Jacob!" Laban shouted. "Nephew! Don't be hasty. I've a mind to be generous today. Just tell me what I should give you."

Softly Jacob said, "Give me nothing. But let me keep for myself those few lambs and kids born spotted or mottled or speckled or striped. Every white sheep shall be yours. Every goat born completely black or brown—yours."

Small sweat popped out on Laban's head, but he restrained his twitching grin. He frowned, murmuring, "Multicolored cattle to you, the rest to me. Hmm." But lambs are nearly always white, and kids all brown or black. Laban, subdued by the stress of this decision, said, "I agree. Keep them that drop speckled from their dams." Then he clapped his hands and cried, "So you'll stay, right? Building your herds? Working for me?"

"Yes."

"Good. It's a beautiful day. Let's go to work."

As soon as Jacob was out of sight, Laban called his sons and commanded them to separate every sheep with the slightest color, every goat with the tiniest white, and drive them away, a full three days' journey away.

That night when he returned from the fields, Jacob met cattle all one color. Not one goat had a star on its forehead, not one ewe showed one hair brown.

One year later—in spring, when Laban, his sons, and all his shepherds were busy shearing their sheep— Jacob's servant found Leah and Rachel among the women, washing the wool.

The servant spoke secretly with them. "Veil your faces," he said, "and follow me. I'll show you where Jacob is."

This was curious. Both wives had assumed that their husband was with the rest of the family. Instead, they were led by a hard route westward, traveling all day till suddenly a valley opened below them, and there they saw huge flocks and herds, and strange people guarding them—and tents! Here were men and women and children, living in tents!

Jacob, bearded and light in a loincloth, strode up the slope of the valley and met them. He put his hands first on Rachel's shoulders and next on Leah's, gazing into their eyes so intently that they felt distressed and wondered what it meant.

He dismissed the servant, then led the women to a massive stone nearby. He himself did not sit.

"Jacob," Leah said, "I've never seen these cattle before, have I?"

"No," he said.

"Are they yours?"

"Yes."

"Does my father know about them?"

Her husband's eyes widened with an agitation Leah hadn't seen before. "No," Jacob said softly, "Laban doesn't know."

Leah turned to Rachel. "Not one animal has a solid color," she said. "See that? They're all speckled or spotted. But they look strong. Jacob, they look very large and strong."

Jacob said, "I have something to say to you. Listen first, then tell me what you think."

The man spoke quietly. There was such appeal in his voice—such concern for their present response—that the women felt a certain strength come into them, and a certain dread.

Jacob said, "Lately I've heard the sons of Laban complain about my presence here. They say I've taken their father's wealth. I think they fear for their own inheritance. On the other hand, I know for a fact that your father has no regard for me anymore. As far east of Haran as we are west of it, there are herds and flocks mottled exactly like these, except that they are weaker than mine. They belong to your father. On the day he promised to give me the multicolored cattle, he removed them all—every goat and sheep—and drove them east.

"You know that I have served him these twenty years with all my strength. Yet he has cheated me. He has changed my wages ten times. What am I to do in such a difficult position?

"I think I have to leave.

"Hush! Rachel, hush a minute. Let me finish."

Jacob knelt down and pulled a shepherd's scrip from under the stone. He opened it and offered each woman a bit of bread. Rachel nibbled at hers. Leah merely held it. Actually, her mouth was dry; but she didn't ask for a drink.

Jacob said, "But God has been with me. I dreamed a thing, and then I did it.

"I took fresh rods of poplar and almond and planed and peeled the bark so the white showed through. Whenever the stronger animals were breeding, I put before their eyes rods white with stripes and speckles and spots. But when the feeble animals bred, I hid the rods. So the mottled kids and the spotted lambs were strong— and they became mine, as you see before you now.

"In that same dream the angel of God said to me, 'Jacob.' I said, 'Here I am.' He said, 'I am the God of Bethel, where you anointed a pillar and made a vow to me. Now arise, go forth from this land and return to the land of your birth.'

"That is what God said, Rachel," Jacob whispered, gazing again with steadfast entreaty into her eyes. "Leah, the Lord God said, Go. What do you think?"

Rachel said, "Let Leah speak. She's older."

Leah said, "I'm thirsty."

Immediately Jacob drew a leather flask from his scrip. She put it to her lips and drank, grateful to find it was wine. Then she handed the flask to Rachel.

"I will tell you the truth," said Leah. "We are treated like foreigners in our father's house. Since we married you, there's been no guarantee that any property will fall to us or to our children hereafter. Now, then, whatever God has said to you, do."

This once, each in the presence of his other wife, Jacob kissed them. Yes: they felt both strength and dread in their souls. They did not feel young any more.

Jacob said, "Prepare the children. Tomorrow your father and brothers are going to shear the sheep they keep three days east of Haran. While they are there, we will steal away to the west."

So Jacob arose and set his family on camels and drove all his cattle westward—all that he had acquired in the land of Paddan-aram.

As his grandfather Abraham had before him, he crossed the Euphrates on inflated goatskins, then turned his face south to the land of Canaan and his father Isaac.

When Laban returned to Haran and saw his great loss, he called his kinsmen together and set out after Jacob. But God came to Laban in a dream by night and said: Take heed that you speak no evil word to Jacob!

Moreover, when he drew near to his nephew, Jacob rode at him in a towering anger. Jacob leveled at Laban a verbal attack so fiery that the older man began to shake.

He said, "These are my daughters. Their children are my children, and the flocks are my flocks. But what can I do this day to these my daughters or to their children? They are in your hand now. Come, let us make a covenant, you and I."

So Jacob took a stone and set it up as a pillar.

They called the pillar Mizpah because it was a watchpost between them. And each man said, "The Lord watch between you and me when we are absent one from the other. And I shall never pass over to you, nor you to me, to do the other harm."

5

South went the long household of Jacob, slowly. In the spring of the year there was good pasturage; but valleys thundered with the flooding rainfall and every small brook swelled into a river.

South, skirting the city of Damascus; south over the high plateau of Bashan, then descending a chalky, limestone land into Gilead; south through that beautiful country where Jacob grew contemplative and withdrew into himself. Here were sights he had not seen in half his lifetime: the western slopes of these hills were rich with olive orchards and vineyards and fields of a young, green grain; the hills themselves were covered in thick forest. Jacob was remembering, overwhelmed with the goodness of Canaan east of the Jordan.

But then they came to the Jabbok River, roaring through its gorges toward the Jordan, and another mood seized Jacob's heart, silencing him altogether.

He had sent messengers to his brother Esau, saying that though he was returning, there was no need for the brothers to meet or intrude on one another's private lives. But the messengers had ridden back at high speeds, crying: "He's coming! Esau is not staying away. He's crossing the Jordan at Jericho and riding north to meet you with four hundred men!"

His brother was coming to kill him. Jacob was afraid.

He led his household down a treacherous path into the Jabbok valley, to the narrow strip of land that ran along the northern bank of the river. There he began to divide his livestock and to send it all ahead of himself in great, successive waves. One wave alone consisted of two hundred and twenty goats, two hundred and twenty sheep, thirty camels, fifty cows and thirty asses—all in the care of several servants whom Jacob commanded to find Esau and say, "This drove of animals belongs to your brother Jacob. He gives them as a present to his lord Esau—and he himself follows behind."

But behind the first wave came a second, the same size, with the same message: "A gift, and your brother follows behind."

In this way Jacob sent a third wave and a fourth, an absolute deluge of wealth, a trick to soften his brother's heart or else to scare him with waves of power.

When his cattle and his drivers had all passed on before him, he saw to it that his wives and their maids and his eleven children likewise went safely over the Jabbok with his most trusted servants.

So then Jacob stood alone on the northern bank of the river: before him the roaring waters; behind him a wall of Nubian sandstone, perpendicular from its foot to the tangled black forest on its brow; right of him there was nothing except a stony, wet plateau; and left of him, nothing.

Night was descending. The gorge grew gloomier, leaving only a path of sky above him, where stars filled the blackness with such tiny lights that he felt small and solitary.

It had been Jacob's intent to make a private crossing of the Jabbok. But maybe he trusted the swimming stroke of his strong arm better in daylight than in the dark; and maybe the night fell faster within the walls of the gorge than he had expected. Whatever the reason, he did not dive into the waters. He did not move. He stood transfixed, surrounded by sound and soon by an absolute darkness—for even the tiny stars were suddenly swallowed as if by a beast of horrible size.

Jacob felt wind, then a chill.

Someone came flying down the riverbank. Jacob felt what he could not see. Then someone attacked him, struck him to the stony ground, and began to wrestle with him. They wrestled by the river. They whirled and heaved each other against the sheer rock wall. In a breathless silence they wrestled all night until a high grey dawn began to streak the sky.

Jacob's adversary touched him in the hollow of his thigh and put his thigh out of joint.

Jacob threw his arm around a huge waist and held on.

The massive foe said, "Let me go, for the day is breaking."

But Jacob shouted, "I will not let you go, unless you bless me."

"What is your name?"

"Jacob."

The contender said, "Your name shall no more be called Jacob, but Israel, for you have striven with God and with men, and have prevailed."

"Who are you?" Jacob cried. "Tell me your name."

But he said, "Why is it that you ask my name?" Then he blessed him and vanished, and he was there no more.

Immediately it was morning.

Jacob tried to rise from the terrible exertions of the night—then suddenly realized whom he had been struggling with all night, even all his life long. He began to tremble.

"I have seen God face-to-face," Jacob whispered, "and yet my life is preserved."

He called the name of that place Peniel: The Face of God.

And the sun rose upon him as he left Peniel, limping because of his thigh.

6

On the morning after God had changed his name to Israel, Jacob looked up and saw Esau approaching with four hundred men.

He did not pause or turn away. He continued walking toward his brother. He limped. Moreover, he kept bowing to the ground in genuine humility.

And when Esau spied Jacob in the distance, he leaped from his donkey and ran as fast as he could to meet him, then fell on his neck and embraced him and kissed him.

Jacob wept because of his brother's kindness.

Both men were bearded. Both beards were shot with white. But Esau's was full and reddish while Jacob's was thin and black. Esau had the stocky body of his uncle Laban. Jacob had the native grace of Rebekah.

Jacob put his hands on Esau's shoulders and smiled. "To see your face is like seeing the face of God because you are receiving me with such favor."

Esau stroked the muscle and the bruises in Jacob's forearm. "You're stronger now," he said. "But, baby brother, your quarrels must be horrible."

Jacob laughed. He begged Esau to keep the presents he had sent him yesterday. And so the brothers were well-met after all. They spent the day together, and then they parted in peace, forever.

Esau returned to Seir, southeast of Canaan, where his family would dwell for centuries thereafter.

Jacob crossed the Jordan River at Succoth and traveled to Shechem. There he made public the name that the Lord God had given him. He purchased a small piece of land and built an altar on it. He called the altar El-Elohe-Israel: God! The God of Israel!

JOSEPH

1

Joseph, the only child of his mother Rachel, was a clever fellow, a boy with a mind of genuine complexity.

"Subtle," his father Jacob would say, tapping his temple. "Levi, why couldn't you learn to count so early?"

Even before he was weaned, Joseph learned that he could cause small explosions in any of his brothers, simply by raising his eyebrows and popping his eyes at the lad. "Stop that!" his brother would yell. "Stop it, you slithering—"

Of course, he only did that trick when their father was present—and then great Jacob would roar the name of the offended brother, "Judah! Judah!" laughing till the tears ran down his nose, utterly stunned by the wit of the infant. "Oh, Judah, the boy drives you like a donkey, doesn't he? Mark my words: he will be someone some day."

No one had the proof, but the brothers believed it was Joseph who told their father about Reuben's sin. Who needed proof? It was always Joseph. He was always sneaking off to tattle.

So one morning Joseph disappeared from the fields where the brothers had led their flocks, and just as they expected, Jacob came out that same afternoon.

"Oh, no," Reuben groaned.

The brothers lifted their eyes, and saw their father striding across the fields like the whirlwind of God, white with wrath. He passed through the flocks as if they were foam, bore down on Reuben, grabbed the young man's staff and began to beat him with it. Backhand, backhand, the big man cracked his son across the buttocks till the rod broke, and Reuben ran for the hills.

When their father departed again, never having uttered the first word, the brothers gaped at each other. What had Reuben done?

Well, Simeon knew. Simeon and Reuben shared the same room in their mother's tent. Three nights ago, with awe and pride and genuine dread, Reuben had described for Simeon his first experience with sex.

"Reuben had sex?" the brothers said.

"Yes," said Simeon.

"That's why father beat him so badly?"

"Well, yes and no. It gets worse."

"What could be worse than that?"

Simeon lowered his voice and said, "Reuben had sex with Bilhah, father's concubine, Rachel's maid—your flesh-mother, Dan, and yours, Naphtali."

All the brothers shivered at this last bit of news. And little lord Joseph!—so he's the one who told it to their father? Yes, and because of him every member of this family now is suffering. It probably never occurred to him what effect his tattling would have on Dan and Naphtali!

What, therefore, should be done about Joseph? What should the brothers do about him?

Reuben got a drubbing—and Joseph got a coat. A dress-coat! A garment so extravagantly long that one could not wear it while working. But then, the little lord never did physical labor anyway.

There was no proof that the coat was a reward for Joseph's witness against Reuben, but everyone assumed it because their father had chosen for his favorite son a coat with the sort of sleeve that only the royalty wore!

Right away the fellow began to dream.

Nor was he private about his dreams. Joseph would don that royal coat and regale the entire family with his dreams, raising his arms for emphasis.

"I dreamed that my brothers and I were binding sheaves in the field," he said. "And lo!"—here he threw up his arms and waved his sleeves—"lo, my sheaf stood upright while my brothers' sheaves bowed down before it."

Did he say bowed? Whoever heard of sheaves bowing like people? Besides, when did the little king actually cut a sheaf in his life?

"I dreamed of the sun and the moon and eleven stars," said Joseph. "And they were all bowing down before me."

Jacob cleared his throat. "This dream is different, isn't it?" he said, frowning. "By sun and moon, can you mean your mother and me?"

One would have wished that Jacob had probed the boy's insolence a little farther. He didn't. And seeing that their father did not, the brothers wondered more and more loudly among themselves: What's to be done with this dreamer?

2

When Joseph was seventeen years old, his mother Rachel became pregnant for the second time in her life. It should have been a year of glad anticipation. But Rachel had ever had a delicate frame; and the same small bones that once had caused such love in Jacob now were frail and uncertain. Her large, lovely eyes were larger now and darker than ever.

Pregnancy made an invalid of Rachel.

Instead of gaining a cushion to soften the child inside of her, there came a month when she actually began to lose weight. Then the baby caused such pain in her pelvis that she had to lie down. Rachel spent the last three months of her term lying on her back. It broke Joseph's heart to see her so.

Whenever he crept into her tent, she smiled and reached to touch his cheek.

"Be good," she said. Often she said, "Joseph, are you befriending your brothers? Do you obey your father's word?"

"Yes," he would say. "Yes."

But then the baby would turn, and she would gasp, and Joseph hurt to see her hurt. Worse, he felt guilty that on his account she should struggle to cover the pain. His presence, then, increased her trouble.

"Be good," she said.

He said, "Yes," and left her alone in the darkness.

Then one night, while Jacob's household was traveling to Ephrath, Joseph was awakened by a long, crimson scream. This was not a lamentation. It was plain animal pain.

Joseph ran outside in time to see his aunt Leah duck into his mother's tent.

He went through the darkness to the back of her tent. He sat down and drew up his legs and wrapped his arms around them. He bit his lip. He bowed his head and rocked because he could hear the sounds his mother was making—woofing sounds, snarling, like the grunting of wild beasts when they tear their prey apart.

Joseph started to cry, but without sobbing. Tears ran down, soaking his robe at the chest.

Toward morning he heard Leah speak in a clear voice. "Don't be afraid, Rachel," she said. "You are bearing another son."

For just an instant Joseph felt almost giddy. Soon it would all be over.

But then he heard the whispering voice of his mother, a ghostly exhalation: Benoni, she breathed. This was her name for the infant. Benoni.

And then she breathed no more.

Joseph tried by the force of his will to make his mother breathe again. He held his own breath. Then someone touched his neck, and he jumped, and it was Leah. She said, "Joseph, go back to bed for a while. I need to speak to your father."

Jacob buried Rachel on the way to Ephrath. He set up a pillar upon her grave.

It is the pillar of Rachel's tomb, which is there to this day, near the village of Bethlehem.

Exactly eight days after he had buried his wife, Jacob circumcised his son. That night he crept into the darkness of Rachel's tent and crouched by her pallet.

He heaved an enormous sigh. Then, suddenly, he smelled her.

He hadn't expected anything like the presence of Rachel to meet him here; but her scent was on the air, something sweet and nourishing, like milk. It was as if the spirit of Rachel herself were passing through the room.

Then it spoke: "But mother named the boy Benoni."

Ah, no, this was not Rachel. It had the lilt and the accent of her voice, but it belonged to Joseph.

Joseph had been here ahead of Jacob, lying in shadows on his own pallet. Perhaps he'd been sleeping here for eight days now.

Jacob turned toward his son and said, "What? What did you say?"

With some emotion Joseph said, "Mother named the boy Benoni. I heard her. But today you circumcised him with another name: Benjamin."

"Yes, yes, I did."

"Why would you change my mother's wishes?"

"How long do you think a people should live with grief, Joseph?"

"I don't know."

"Always? Do you think Rachel would want us forever to grieve?"

"No."

"And your brother, how long should he be sorrowful? He will never be able to remember his mother or his birth. Do you think his mother would want him to go in gloom through the rest of his life?"

"No."

"No, surely she wouldn't. But Benoni means The Son of My Sorrow. And Benjamin means The Son of My Right Hand. Joseph, your mother was sad for a little while, and now she is sad no more. She named the birth. She named the pain. She named the moment and the coming of her son, and we will remember the name, you and I. This will be a covenant between us, together to remember the name Benoni and all that it stood for. She named the birth; let us name the boy. Why shouldn't your brother bear the brightness of his mother's more lasting character? Why shouldn't he carry her confidence into his life and into the world? Her right hand. My right hand. Our . . .

"Oh, Joseph, hush," Jacob said. "My dear son, all is well now. The Lord is with us. Hush, hush."

For Joseph had taken his father's hand and had laid the palm against his face, and now the older man could feel the wetness on his boy's chin. Joseph was crying.

So then they held each other, smelling Rachel's scent. And Jacob talked long into the night telling his son of the past, his love for Rachel, his wrestlings with God, his trust in the Lord God, the behavior that the Lord loves—and the covenant that had kept them safe through all these years.

One morning while Jacob and his household were sojourning in the valley of Hebron, he called Joseph to himself and said, "My son, even your baby brother is smiling today. It's time to put your sorrow aside. Be busy. Talk to others. Listen to them. Share interests.

"Come, now," he said with cheer. "Your brothers are pasturing the flocks at Shechem, several days away. Go there, Joseph, to see whether it is well with them and with the flocks, then bring me word again."

In fact, it was the season for pleasant weather, after the rains but before the summer sun grew hot. And old Jacob knew from his own experience how pleasant a lazy trip north could be.

He sincerely wished to lift the spirits of his son; and he felt he was succeeding when Joseph came to say good-bye, wearing his gorgeous coat. It filled Jacob's heart with gratitude to see his son dressed thus. Yes, the coat had been an extravagance; but as long as it made the lad happy, it was worth the cost.

"Go safely," Jacob said, kissing Joseph and noticing that they stood on a level now. The child had grown as tall as his father.

"I will," said Joseph. Then he called out, "Where's my big brother Benjamin?"

Leah brought Benjamin out, and Jacob watched with tenderness while Joseph rained kisses on the baby, causing him to bark a husky laughter. Then the whole company was laughing, Jacob and Joseph and Benjamin and Leah.

Yes, yes, grief was coming to its conclusion.

"Good-bye, Joseph. God be with you, my son. Good-bye."

"And with you, Father. Good-bye."

Seven days later, when the ten grown sons of Jacob returned from Shechem, Joseph was not among them. No, they hadn't seen him. They swore they hadn't seen Joseph anywhere since they had left Hebron more than a month ago.

On the other hand, they'd found a coat. A coat with long sleeves, very similar to Joseph's. Stiff with dried blood. It had been torn violently in three places.

"Father, can it be Joseph's coat?"

The old man took one look at the riven cloth and began to howl. "My son! My son!" he wailed. He tried to smooth the garment with the flat of his hand, then gathered it up and buried his face in it. "My son has been devoured by lions," he cried. "Surely Joseph is torn to pieces!"

Jacob rent his robe and put sackcloth upon his loins and mourned many days.

Reuben and Simeon and Levi and Dinah—all his children, one by one—came to his tent and tried to comfort him. But Jacob refused to be comforted. He said, "No, no—I will go to my grave lamenting Joseph, lamenting my dear son Joseph."

3

But in the same days when the old man began to mourn the death of his son, Joseph was walking among the camels. He went in the midst of a caravan which followed an ancient trade route southwest along the coast of the Great Sea past Gaza, then west across the northern portion of Sinai to Goshen and into Egypt.

He went manacled neck and ankle. He was chained in line with twenty other men of several languages and various countries. His feet were bleeding.

His captors were not wicked. Nor were they merciful. They were merchants. Together with other goods—gum and balm and myrrh—they meant to sell the sleek young man at a profit. They had purchased him for twenty shekels, a reasonable price for a healthy male; but Egyptian coin would increase the investment, as long as he was healthy still when they got to that country. Therefore, they did not begrudge him bread. All their slaves improved in the passage. It was a matter of pride.

Joseph had actually felt happy to see his brothers and their flocks spread out in a valley below him. They had been a surprising vision as he came over a grassy rise—and the lightness of his spirit at the sight had likewise surprised him. Yes, he had been lonely too long, too long mourning his mother.

"Brothers!" he called, grinning and waving. "Brothers, I am here!"

As he descended the slope in a little trot, he saw that they were gathering together and looking his way.

But they were not smiling.

Naphtali said, "The dreamer."

At this distance Joseph couldn't be sure, but it seemed that Naphtali had spat the word. His mouth looked twisted. Then Dan shouted with bloody savagery, "Let's see what becomes of his dreams," and Joseph slowed his step.

Two of the brothers, then three, then five broke from the group, running as fast as they could in Joseph's direction. All of the brothers were shouting now, all ten of them. Joseph's throat tightened. It felt as if he were in a dream. He absolutely could not move, trying and trying to make some sense of the moment.

Then his brothers were on him, whirling him around and ripping the long coat from his body. Someone hit him a solid blow to the side of his head. Joseph observed the impact and the pain with astonishment. There was meaning in that blow. Someone struck him in the small of his back and he crumpled. Then they were dragging him by his legs over dirt and rock, and then the earth opened up beneath him and he was falling. He hit bottom in an echoing place. He made an odd croaking sound. The wind was knocked out of him. He couldn't breathe. He glanced up and saw a small hole, the heads of his brothers blocking sunlight, then sank into unconsciousness. He was in a cistern. The thought accompanied him into the utter darkness: I'm in a cistern. But I am not dead. I am in a cistern. O Lord, be with me now.

Joseph had not died. Instead, he was sold to slave traders; and two months later he found himself standing on a whitewashed platform, listening to the foreign tongues around him. The platform was surrounded by men with neat beards, trimmed to an oiled tuft at the chin. Some had side-whiskers from ear to jaw, but no one wore the sort of cheek-bushes he was used to. Men must pluck their hairs. And everyone, it seemed, bathed. Joseph couldn't smell sweat. People wore white linen in this country, a fabric as supple and smooth as human flesh. A marvel, nothing at all as rough as the wool he knew.

Clearly he was in a marketplace.

And those that stood on the platform were for sale.

To the left of the platform Joseph saw a small operation which caused him to become excited. Egyptians sat on chairs: here was a man sitting up on a chair behind a flat surface of wood. A table. And on that table was unrolled another sort of fabric altogether, stronger than linen. The man was making marks on that fabric with astonishing speed. For every slave sold, he would dip an instrument in black water, then form a series of swift, exquisite shapes on the fabric. Joseph peered more closely: the instrument was made from a rush that had been cut on a slant and frayed at the end, a brush for black ink! Joseph had heard of writing before. His father had explained to him the anonymous marks in clay and old stone. But this was a miracle of speed and simplicity, and it delighted him.

Before the bidding began for him particularly, Joseph realized one other wonderful fact about the man who wrote with rushes: that he was himself a slave.

Therefore, when the auctioneer asked him what skills he could perform, Joseph answered by pointing at the scribe on his left. "That," he said. "I can do that." In his soul he said, Or if I cannot do it, I can learn.

And if anyone had questioned him further, wondering how he knew the scribe was a slave or where he got the gall to say he knew the crafts of a nimble mind, Joseph would without hesitation have answered: "The Lord is with me."

It happened that the man who purchased Joseph was a figure of importance in the land of Egypt. His name was Potiphar, "the one whom Re has given": Re, the sun-god of the Egyptians.

Potiphar held the rank of captain, commanding Pharaoh's personal guard. He carried—perhaps as a mere honorific, perhaps as a fact—the title "Eunuch," though he was married to a woman who was, said the royal gossip, both young and vital. Potiphar himself, despite his power, was not a physically imposing presence. On the other hand, his tiny eyes were shrewd and sure, as accurate as darts and as dangerous. He rode through the city, well-oiled, sweet-smelling, bejeweled, and revered wherever he went. He returned to a house built high above the river, a proud palatial edifice of marble-white walls, interior courtyards, many rooms, fountains outside, baths within, latticed windows to shape the light, and floors inlaid with bold mosaic. But the beauty above hid an official cruelty below. The captain of Pharaoh's guard was also the lord of his prisons, and Pharaoh's prisons were the basement chambers of the captain's house.

At Potiphar's insistence, every slave and servant wore linen as rich as his own. He wanted his household to reflect well upon his position and his evident generosity. Joseph, therefore, regularly washed his entire body with warm water and dressed himself in two pieces of clothing: the first an undergarment worn at all times, a long soft shirt tied about the hips; the second an elegant, close-fitting cape for wearing in public places.

In fact, Joseph seldom needed the cape. Potiphar kept him close to home because he genuinely liked the Hebrew.

This slave smiled. There was nothing cringing or fawning about him, but with good health and a glad disposition he would look his master straight in the eye and smile. What other slave was so peaceful in his position as to befriend the lofty Potiphar? None. And besides all that, it was a handsome, manly smile.

Joseph learned to write Egyptian as well as he spoke it, because he learned both skills at once. And swiftly— before the end of his first year in this master's service— the Hebrew had proven to be more than competent. Many accountants were competent; few were also trust-worthy. On impulse, once, Potiphar asked Joseph to inventory the goods of the household. When he was done, nothing was missing, not so much as a finger's breadth of wheat from the bins; but measures that had been falsified on previous lists now came to light. The Hebrew slave revealed these thefts without criticism or self-righteousness. He managed to make it a proper, impersonal report.

Therefore, Potiphar appointed Joseph to be overseer of his entire household. And then he was delighted to dis-cover that his properties, his harvests and investments, and even the transactions of the household, prospered.

"How is it you succeed so well?" he asked the slave. "And how can you take such pleasure in my prosperity."

The Hebrew replied with a smile, "God is with me."

God was with him. And this, to him, was the proof: that even as a stranger in a foreign land, Joseph had come to enjoy the daily routine of his life.

Early in the morning he entered the room from which he conducted his master's business. There, look-ing out an eastern window, he did as he had seen his father do—he gave thanks to God. Then he removed his cape, sat down in an Egyptian chair before an Egyptian table, mixed the inks and cut the rushes for his writing.

Within the hour Potiphar would arrive to discuss the day's projects, to receive reports, to give advice, and to ask for it. After their conference, the master left for Pharaoh's court, while the slave stayed home and worked. So went his days. So passed the seasons, wet and dry.

Soon Potiphar's wife also began to bring various small tasks of her own into Joseph's room. He always rose to greet her. She always gave him a dead-level gaze and a thin smile. Though Potiphar was short, his wife was exactly Joseph's height. She would let him hold the tips of her fingers a moment, then she said, "Come, come, no need to be so formal."

But Joseph was never anything less than formal. It was more than his natural manner; it was a conscious choice. Often he went out to make purchases for the household. "Here is my seal," Potiphar had said to him. "If you think we need it, buy it. I trust your judgment." And since he acted in his master's name, it seemed right to act in self-effacing formality.

In a self-effacing formality, then, Joseph always waited until his master's wife was seated before he sat again to write.

She was, however, a perplexing woman. Clearly, her eye was lit with an interior intelligence. She could comport herself with a majestic dignity. Yet sometimes she would, exactly like a child, jump up the moment Joseph sat down, forcing him to rise again with embarrassment. It seemed to him she was testing the truth of his courtesy. He could be patient for whims of his mistress, of course; but it interrupted his work.

One day while she was sitting some distance away from his table, the woman began to murmur words so softly he scarcely heard them. He thought she was singing to herself. But suddenly he caught the words,

Hebrew, lie with me, and his ears burst into flame. Joseph did not look up. Maybe he had imagined the phrase, for as soon as he heard it, she fell into a perfect silence. And after a moment she rose and left the room.

Joseph released a long, trembling sigh.

Three days later they happened again to be in the room alone.

Potiphar's wife said, "Joseph?"

He looked up.

She was gazing at him from dead-level eyes, the lids made green with malachite. "Joseph," she said. "Lie with me."

He gaped. Her neck was extraordinarily long, her throat naked.

Softly she said, "Did you hear me? Do you understand?"

Without a word he stood up, pulled on his cape, walked out of the room and through the courtyard and out of the house altogether.

When she entered the room on the following day, precisely at her usual time, Joseph rose as always to greet her, but he kept his eyes cast down and he did not take her hand. Neither did she reach for his. Nor did she sit. There was a servant standing at the door. She dismissed him.

So then they stood alone, his eyes lowered, hers burning the flesh of his forehead.

"Joseph," she said, "do you know what I want?"

"Yes," he said.

"Then why did you walk away from me yesterday?"

Now he looked at her. He wished he weren't panting like a child, but he had to speak: "My master," he said, then paused to breathe. "My master trusts me with everything he has—everything, my lady, except yourself, because you are his wife. How, then, can I do this great wickedness and sin against God?"

Potiphar's wife said nothing. Her lips drew thin and tight across her teeth. Her silences could be terrible. Perhaps she would leave now. Instead, abruptly, she sat. Joseph sat down, too. He tried to write. But every time he flicked up his eyes, he saw that she was staring at him in a cold silence.

Then she was gone. For ten days Joseph worked in his room alone.

But on the afternoon of the eleventh day, the woman appeared in the doorway, her hair loose, her eye unpainted, bright and wild. "Slaves," she hissed, "know nothing of gods and sin! Don't you ever pretend to be better than me!" She strode into the room. Joseph started to stand. She rushed at him and grabbed his undergarment at the shoulders. "Lie with me," she cried. "Hebrew, lie with me!"

Joseph rose up and pushed her backward. She fell against a cabinet filled with scrolls. But she was clinging to his garment. It ripped at the seam and came off. Joseph stood for an instant completely naked, then he leaped from the room and ran out into the courtyard blinded by his shame.

"Get off me! Get off me!" The woman was screaming inside the house. "Help! Help! The slave is trying to rape me! Help!"

Joseph whirled around. He saw Potiphar's wife stepping calmly through the doorway, though her mouth was open and she was making a powerful screaming sound. In her hand was his undergarment, in her eyes a cold, emotionless ice.

All at once there bounded from the door behind her four large Egyptian men, very angry. Joseph didn't try to run. Where would he go, naked? Nor did he fight back.

He was beaten to the ground. He was struck on the back of his skull with the flat of someone's sword. Gratefully, then, he passed out.

Joseph awoke in Potiphar's basement—the prisons of the captain of Pharaoh's guard.

The walls were thick. The rooms were narrow and dark and mostly bare. There were many such rooms, a labyrinth of rooms inhabited by men of every rank. Joseph discovered a hidden community of unfortunate men, none of whom knew when he might be released since there were no fixed sentences. There was only the whim of the powerful people upstairs.

But even the netherworld was arranged like the world in light: prisoners who came down from high positions were served by prisoners who came from no position at all.

When two officers of Pharaoh's court were cast into these chambers—each for some offense which their lord must soon have forgotten—Joseph was charged to serve them. One was Pharaoh's butler. The other had been his baker. But Joseph was a Hebrew; therefore, they took his ministrations for granted and ignored him.

Time passed and neither courtier heard word from on high regarding his release. Each man sank into despair. They experienced horrible bouts of anxiety. And because slaves are nonentities, they confided their feelings to the Hebrew.

"What can we do to survive in here?" they asked. "Tell us," they begged, "how you endure this misery."

But the slave only said, "The Lord is with me."

One morning, as Joseph approached the cell of his masters with water and cloths to wash them, he heard an odd, choked moaning. When he entered, he found both

Egyptians crouched in corners, shivering, holding their elbows as if cold to the bone. They were staring at the floor with gaunt eyes.

Joseph said, "What is the matter with you?"

The butler leaped to his feet and pressed his hands to his temples. "Hebrew, Hebrew, what do you know about us?" he cried. He turned to the wall. "We dreamed last night. Both of us. But there's no one in this pit to interpret the dreams. You have no idea, the agony. But it's not your fault. You've never lived as we have. Wash me and go away."

The delicate man sat down, tilted his head upward and closed his eyes.

Joseph wet his cloth and began to wash the butler's ears. "I have dreamed," he said softly. "And my dreams had meanings. Very good meanings, so I thought at the time. But no one had to interpret my dreams to me."

"What do you mean?" The butler opened one eye.

"I knew the meanings the moment I awoke."

The butler opened both eyes. "How? Are you a magician?"

"Don't all interpretations belong to God?" said Joseph. "And where is God not? God is everywhere."

The baker, much smaller than the butler, more private by profession, crept up to Joseph and touched his shoulder.

"Here?" the baker whispered. "God is . . . here?"

"Everywhere," said Joseph.

"Do you think," the baker whispered with dreadful hesitation, "that God would perhaps be willing to interpret our dreams?"

Suddenly the butler seized both of Joseph's wrists. "Listen! Listen to this," he hissed and then launched into a breathless monologue: "I saw a grapevine with three branches, budding. Its blossoms burst open, and immediately there were clusters of ripe grapes, and I was pressing the grapes into Pharaoh's cup which was in my hand, and then I was taking the wine to him. What does your God think it means?"

Joseph plucked the butler's fingers from around his wrists, moistened the cloths and turned to the baker.

"The three branches are three days," Joseph said, beginning to wash the baker's face. "In three days Pharaoh will raise your head from here to himself above. He will restore you to your former office as his butler." Joseph turned to look at the butler. "This is the true meaning. When it takes place, remember me. When you are in Pharaoh's presence once again, please tell him of my situation. I beg you to ask for clemency."

Now, even the soft-spoken baker could not sit still. He wriggled beneath Joseph's hand, so Joseph touched the man's brow with the cloth and said, "What was your dream?"

The baker closed his eyes. "I dreamed that there were three baskets on my head. The topmost basket carried cakes for Pharaoh, but the birds were pecking them. That is all."

The man fell silent. Joseph likewise said nothing for a long time. He washed the baker all down his arms, and when he came to the hands, he lingered.

"The three baskets are three days," he said. "In three days Pharaoh will raise your head from—" Joseph folded the man's hands within his own. "— will raise your head from your shoulders," he said. "He will hang you on a tree. The birds will eat the flesh from you."

In three days the Pharaoh chose to celebrate his birthday by means of a feast for all his servants. On that occasion he remembered the butler and the baker, officers he had consigned to prison. The butler he brought back into his palace and his good graces. The baker he hanged.

But the butler forgot how he came to know the fortune that befell him.

So Joseph was in prison. In the dark pit of prison Joseph lay down on rotten bullrushes, while the days passed into months and the months into years.

4

Pharaoh slept on a couch. During the day it was a divan for sitting; at night it became his bed.

In the company of several wakeful servants, Pharaoh slept on a couch which was crafted of cedar and gold and silver. It was covered with thicknesses of linen; it was set on a raised pavement, itself a splendid mosaic of porphyry, marble, mother-of-pearl, and other precious stones.

And the king of Egypt slept in light.

Oil lamps burned while Pharaoh was sleeping. Water flowed near his private chamber, murmuring softly, ready to slake or wash or cool the body of the king.

Curtains of a dark and curious weave stilled any wind that wandered the palace; rugs softened any step; and music could, if necessary, immediately comfort any nightmare; a harp and a lute waited to be brushed by the fingers of young girls. Likewise, a priest was never far away. Pharaoh was blood-kin to the gods. He slept attended. He slept in the company of many ministers. And yet this sacred personage slept on his beautiful couch in a loneliness deeper than any.

This was not so much his will as it was his station. It could not be changed.

One night Pharaoh lunged awake with a cry, staring about himself as if blind. His bedclothes fell aside.

Straightway two servants rushed in with moist towels. Young girls touched their instruments, causing shy chords to catch the air. A woman moved through the room brightening every lamp. Another brought new linen covers for the king's body.

Soon Pharaoh lay back and fell again into a fitful sleep.

But he mumbled and sweated and threw his arms about so that the servants who crept too close to fan him got cuffed.

Again the king lunged awake, panting and staring into the air.

"Where is the priest?" he cried. "Bring me the priest!"

The priest was already beside him, with a flask of wine and a silver cup.

Pharaoh gripped his arm. The cup splashed wine down the skirts of the priest.

Pharaoh said, "I dreamed. I dreamed a dreadful dream. I dreamed two dreams, very similar, very significant, very—"

Without releasing the priest's arm, Pharaoh told his dreams in sacred awe and in precise detail.

"What do they mean?" he said.

The poor priest had turned white during the recitation. Yes, the dreams were clearly heavy with meaning. So much the worse for the priest, who hadn't the first idea what they meant.

"Then bring me the magi!" the king commanded. "I want those who have made a profession of the sciences! Let them study this and interpret it!"

Pharaoh then recounted his dreams to a series of grave, thoughtful men, students of the universe. Courtly men pretended interpretations—and enraged the king. "You take me for a fool?" he cried. Men of honor bowed their heads and admitted failure. Men frightened even to approach the foot of Pharaoh stood gaping and mute.

"Is that it? Have I met every wise head in the kingdom? Is there no one to interpret my dreams to me?"

Then it was that the chief butler received his memory again. "O Pharaoh," he said, "There was a Hebrew slave in prison who interpreted my dream for me. He told me that my dream spoke of you, sir—that you would elevate me to your service again. And he was right."

"What is this Hebrew's name?"

"I never knew. Sir, I never knew his name."

It was the captain of the king's own guard, Potiphar, who ushered into Pharaoh's presence a Hebrew man thirty years old, newly shaven, pale from the prisons, but confident in his carriage and level in his looking.

Pharaoh regarded the slave, who nodded and smiled.

"Hebrew, do you interpret dreams?"

"No," said the slave without embarrassment. "It isn't in me to interpret dreams. But God does. God can give an answer to Pharaoh concerning his dreams."

"Hebrew," Pharaoh said, slowly measuring the man from his foot to his face, "what is your name?"

"Joseph. I am the son of Jacob, who is called Israel."

"Joseph, then," Pharaoh said, "these are my dreams."

"I was standing by the Nile when seven cows, sleek and fat, climbed out of the water and began to graze on the reed grass. Immediately seven other cows came out. These were sickly cattle, very thin. They swallowed down the fat cows, and yet they stayed as thin as before. I woke from that dream, then slept and dreamed again.

"I saw seven ears of grain, plump and good, all growing on a single stalk. But then there sprouted seven more ears, thin and blighted by the east wind. Exactly as in my first dream, the thin ears ate the full ears.

"Joseph, son of Jacob, what does it mean?"

The Hebrew's expression had grown solemn. His voice now came soft with humility and perfect certitude. "God has shown Pharaoh what he is about to do through many lands," he said. "The seven good cows and the seven good ears are seven years. Your dreams are one. There will be seven years of great plenty in Egypt. But then the lean cows and the blighted ears stand for seven years of famine to follow the abundant years. Famine shall consume the kingdom so grievously that the time of plenty will be forgotten altogether. And the doubling of Pharaoh's dream means that the thing is fixed by God. It will surely be."

For a moment the halls of the Pharaoh were still. No one spoke, neither priest nor butler, wise man, or eunuch or slave. The king and the Hebrew looked at one another.

It was Joseph who broke silence.

"If Pharaoh wishes," he said, "I have a suggestion."

"Speak."

"Let Pharaoh appoint someone discreet, impartial, and wise to administer a gathering of grain during the seven years of plenty. Let granaries be built in which to store food against the seven years of famine that are to follow."

Two sentences. The Hebrew had uttered in two sentences such a clear common sense that Pharaoh stood up, stepped down from his dais, and confronted the man on an equal level, eye to eye.

"What would you say, Joseph? Shouldn't my administrator also exhibit the spirit of God? Shouldn't he be both bold and honorable?"

The Hebrew said, "Yes."

"Yes," said Pharaoh. "Yes, and since God is with you, interpreting dreams and offering prompt, impeccable counsel, I choose you."

The king of Egypt turned to a messenger and framed a decree to go forth through the entire kingdom:

"Watch, Philopater," he said. "Do you see how I put my signet ring on this man's hand?"

The messenger nodded.

"Yes, you have seen it," said the king. "Joseph, the son of Jacob, now has power to issue orders in the king's name and the ring to seal the same. He is no slave. He is no prisoner. He is under the authority of none but me, and all are under his authority. Mark it: he is my governor.

"Watch, Philopater. Do you see how I array the man in royal robes the like of my own? Do you see how I hang a golden chain around his neck? Yes, and when he rides through the kingdom, it shall be in a chariot whose glory rivals mine. And you, Philopater, shall command runners to go before him, crying, "Abrek! Abrek! Kneel before the governor's passing!'"

And so it was.

Pharaoh gave his new governor a new name: Zaphenath-paneah. By this name his fame went forth throughout Egypt and yet farther to the kingdoms north and east. Zaphenath-paneah, the Man who Lives when the Deity Speaks.

So God was with Joseph.

He married Asenath, the daughter of the priest of On, and was comforted with human companionship.

Moreover, by the wisdom which God had invested in him, he accomplished the tasks he himself had recommended to the king. Joseph oversaw the building of spacious granaries. Then, during the plenteous years, he gathered so much food that finally it could no longer be measured.

During those years, too, his wife bore him two sons. Joseph called the first Manasseh. It meant Making To Forget. For he said, "God has caused me to forget my hardship."

The second child he called Ephraim, To Be Fruitful. For in the evenings Joseph would ascend to a high window in his house and gaze down at the river valley, the fields, the crops of his adopted country: his life. And what was all this land, by the hand of God, if not fruitful?

But soon, exactly as the Lord God had communicated unto Pharaoh, the earth withered and hardened and cracked. Its plenty came to an end. Even the mighty Nile shrank and could not serve the soil. Famine began.

Months of drought became years of drought, so that the people despaired of rain and harvests. They ground dust between their teeth. It was a famine indeed.

As governor, Joseph opened the granaries slowly, sparingly. He knew he had to dole out their stores through seven years. The Egyptians, therefore, did not eat much. But they ate. And they did not die.

5

Old Jacob stood on a hill near Hebron, squinting across a stony gorge to the ridge road that traveled north and south in that region.

"See that?" he said. He raised his hand and pointed toward a file of travelers toiling along the ridge. They were silhouettes in a slow dance northward. Jacob's eyes watered in the dying sunlight.

"You see that lot?" he said. "They are tired, but their sacks are full. They are poorer, but they will eat for three months."

Jacob leaned heavily on a staff. He was speaking to his fourth son, Judah, who stood stout and strong beside him. This one was as quiet as his mother Leah. Once Jacob had mistrusted the child of his who did not talk. Now he believed that Judah's silences came of conviction and not of deceit.

"I think it is time we did the same," he said. "How many goats still give milk? There is neither milk nor cheese left. The rams live and the ewes die and even the lambs that are born die when their dams do. Judah?"

"Here I am, father."

"When did the last merchant caravan pass this way?"

"More than three years ago."

"Who travels through these dead lands?"

"Thieves. Gangs. The famished."

"Yes, and city-delegations to Egypt to buy grain. Those travelers there are proof that the rumors are true. Egypt has food, and it is time we went as well." The old man turned to face his son directly. "Take your brothers for protection. Leave your wives and children with me. Go down to Egypt and barter the best you can. Buy grain and come home again with full sacks."

Judah continued to gaze toward the sunset. His face took a bronze tinge. He had a broad forehead and a large nose. Jacob admired the nose on his son, but he wished the expression were more mobile. Judah's features chiefly showed restraint and rectitude.

"Father."

"Yes?"

"All my brothers?"

"No!" Jacob shouted. His stomach contracted. He gripped the staff for stability. Then, with more control, he said, "No, not Benjamin. All but Benjamin. Benjamin stays with me."

Soon Judah and his brothers, their donkeys, provisions, weapons and wealth, crossed to the ridge road themselves, where they turned south and slowly rode away, while Jacob and his youngest child stood watching the departure.

The old man put his arm around the boy. Benjamin was fourteen years old. He had a tangle of beautiful hair. He was a mere baby.

The rainy season passed without rain. Only a few light showers fell to taunt the starving tribes.

Jacob went out every day to watch for the return of his sons. Every day was clear and hot. His old eyes could see very far across the land.

And then one afternoon he recognized their dark forms in the distance, so he hurried back to the tents to prepare a meal for their arrival.

They ate a solemn feast. The eating preceded any talking. Jacob kept jumping up and looking south. Ten of his sons had gone into Egypt. Only nine returned. Simeon had not come back. Judah grimly avoided his father's glances—and Jacob could scarcely stand the silence.

Finally he broke the ceremony of their feasting and cried, "Where's Simeon? What happened to Simeon? Why hasn't my second son come back?"

All the brothers ceased eating and sat in grave silence.

Judah said, "The grand vizier of Egypt, the most powerful officer, second only to Pharaoh, the governor

in charge of foodstores—Zaphenath-paneah himself—
required that Simeon stay behind in prison."

Jacob held onto his staff with both hands, or else
he would surely have collapsed. He was the only one
standing. His sons sat with their heads hung down, grizzled hair and sorrow covering their faces.

"Why? Judah, why? Why would the governor want
Simeon? What crime did he commit?"

"The grand vizier," said Judah, "charged us all with
a crime. All of us. He said we were spies."

"What? Spies? What did you do?"

"We don't know." Stout Judah now raised his face
and looked helplessly at his father. "We were surprised
that the man wanted to see us at all.

"Father," Judah said, "there are many people in
Egypt to buy food, and there are officers to handle the
traffic. But the governor himself came out to look at us.
He asked where we came from. We said Canaan. He
asked who our father was. We said, Jacob, called Israel.
Then he said, Yes, well, you are spies. He accused us of
spying. We said, No, we are brothers, plain shepherds.
We told him there was no one else in Canaan except our
father and one other brother.

"What is your brother's name? he asked.

"Benjamin, we said.

"The governor grew very angry then. We don't
know the cause of his anger. Father, we could not understand this Egyptian. Benjamin? he said. We said, Yes,
Benjamin.

"Then he said, Bring Benjamin here, and I will
know that you are not spies."

At these words, Jacob slumped to the ground.
Reuben rushed to catch him. Reuben and Levi together
cradled the man while Benjamin ran for a flask of water.

Judah watched unmoving. There was the tightness of genuine anguish in his face.

"What else?" Jacob whispered, lying in the lap of his sons.

Judah spoke softly. "We told him we could not bring Benjamin. We said it would kill you. We said you had already lost one son and could not lose another. The grand vizier only seemed to grow more furious as we talked. His face was white. His voice was a whisper. He spoke Egyptian, but the translator said, 'Then you shall stay in prison till one of you goes to Canaan and brings Benjamin here.'

"So we sat in prison for three days. Then the governor came and said, I've changed my mind.' He pointed at Simeon. 'That one stays. The rest of you, go and come back with Benjamin. Your food is already in sacks on the backs of your beasts,' he said. 'Go.'

"And so we have come."

In order to show that their journey had done some good, the brothers brought forth their sacks of grain and opened them.

But there arose into the night sky a howl of extremest sorrow. For old Jacob saw in each sack of his sons the money he had sent for payment. "What are you doing to me?" he cried. "You have stolen from the governor of Egypt! No, no, no, no, no, you will not take the son of my right hand into such danger. I am sorry for Simeon—but you will not bring my grey head down in sorrow to the grave."

In the year that followed, no green thing grew for forage. Judah watched as the flocks and herds of his father sickened and died. People did not have the strength to drag the carcasses away.

Judah thought often of his brother languishing in an Egyptian prison. Simeon. Perhaps he was eating, but he was not here. Nevertheless, sins lay heavy on Judah's soul. And the pain of his father shut his mouth. He would not speak.

But when their previous stores of grain were gone, when his children and Jacob's grandchildren grew gaunt, and when their bellies distended with hunger, his father came into his tent and said, "Judah, go again. Try to buy a little food again from Egypt."

Judah said, "Father, sit down and listen to me."

He held his peace till Jacob sighed and sat. Perhaps the old man knew what was coming.

Then Judah said, "The grand vizier in Egypt solemnly warned us, saying: You will not see my face unless your brother is with you. Now, then, if you send Benjamin along, we will go. But if you won't, we cannot go to Egypt."

Jacob said, "How could you do this wickedness against me, telling the man I had another son?"

Judah said, "He questioned us closely. We only answered his questions."

Judah waited a moment in silence. Then he said, "Father, you know that we all will die if we don't do something now. Everyone will die. You and all your children and all our little ones. But send Benjamin with me and I will be surety for him. If I do not bring him back, let me bear the blame forever."

Long, long Jacob sat in silence.

Finally he said, "A little balm. A little wild honey." He pulled himself up by grabbing his staff. He limped to the door of the tent and turned. "Take gum to the governor and myrrh and pistachio nuts and almonds. Take double the money to pay for both loads of food." The old man turned away. He stood in the doorway staring out at the dusk, an ancient shadow, an enormous sorrow. "And," he whispered, "take your brother Benjamin."

The chief steward of the grand vizier brought his master news at noon of a bright blue day: that the same men who had come from Canaan last year now had returned again.

"You wished to be informed," he said.

"Yes," said Joseph. He was in his working room in Pharaoh's palace. "How many are there?"

"Ten, my lord. I think ten."

Joseph felt his heart beat faster. "Wait for them in the marketplace," he said to the steward. "When they arrive, take them straight to my house. Slaughter an animal. Prepare a feast. I will share my evening meal with them."

By a stern self-discipline Joseph spent the day attending to his regular affairs.

Nevertheless, he placed himself near a latticed window from which he could watch the sons of Jacob. He saw his steward step forward to meet them. He watched the exchange of greetings—and then their faces fell, troubled by his invitation. Twice the steward tried to lead them to the governor's house, high on a hill; twice he had to turn back and beg them to follow. But all at once the men opened their pitiful sacks, pulled out a great deal of money, spread it on the ground and gesticulated, loudly explaining something. The good steward only put the money back again, grabbed their sacks himself, and in this way persuaded them to follow.

Next Joseph ordered Simeon's release. He, too, was led to the vizier's private quarters.

Then, late in the day, Joseph himself walked home.

As he approached his courtyard he heard a babble of Hebrew voices: "Simeon! Simeon, is it you? How are you? Oh, Simeon, how did they treat you?"

And Simeon's voice: "How is father? Oh, no! Reuben, you brought Benjamin—"

Joseph felt such a constriction in his throat that he feared he could not speak. Benjamin is here!

He strode into the courtyard and with a hard tone said, "How is your father? Is he alive?"

The brothers immediately fell on their faces before him. His interpreter repeated the question in Hebrew, but the brothers didn't move.

Joseph barked, "Stand up!" The interpreter didn't have to repeat it. The men rose slowly, gazing at Joseph with genuine fear. Wordlessly they pushed pots and jars toward him, balm and honey and gum and almonds.

Joseph said, "The old man of whom you told me, Jacob, Israel—is he well?"

In Hebrew the brothers murmured, "Your servant our father is alive. Yes, and he is well."

The breath was squeezed in Joseph's chest. Suddenly he saw the fourteen-year-old Benjamin, the image of their mother Rachel, a remarkable fall of dark hair—and then Joseph couldn't breathe at all. His face flamed with emotion. His nostrils flared. He pinched his lips and frowned like thunder. The brothers shrank backward from him. Joseph whispered, "This is your youngest brother?"

Judah stared at the governor. "Yes," he said. "Benjamin."

Joseph said, "Benjamin—"

But the name on his lips undid him. He covered his face and rushed from the courtyard into an inner room, where he burst into tears and wept: Benjamin.

During the meal that followed, Joseph watched how furtively his brothers ate. Eleven brothers: their hunger must be violent within them, but their fear must be greater. They nibbled. He sent them enormous portions. He sent Benjamin five times what he sent the others. Still, everyone only nibbled.

To his chief steward he whispered, "Go out and fill the sacks of the Hebrews with food and with their own money again. All of it." He pointed at Benjamin. "And in the sack of the lad place my silver cup. Go."

Speaking through the interpreter, Joseph required the shepherds to spend the night in his own quarters, then he left them.

He did not sleep at all that night.

Immediately at sunrise the following morning he heard the commotion of men preparing to leave. He ascended to the high window of his house and watched them go with haste and fear and elation. Eleven of them. Without turning around, he spoke to the steward waiting behind them.

"Follow them," he said. "Block their progress. Ask why they would repay the vizier evil for good. Ask for my silver cup. Make them open their sacks. Call him who has the cup a thief, and bring him here."

Joseph watched his servant ride forth in a magnificent chariot, approach his brothers, command them to halt, command them to open their sacks. He watched the terror thicken in his brothers' faces as money fell out before the grain. And then, when the silver cup rolled out of Benjamin's sack, he saw how the ten older brothers all took hold of their robes and tore them. They made a terrible wailing. He could hear it even here, on his hill, in his house, behind the lattice of his window.

He watched them slowly retrace their steps, returning to the house again.

He was sitting on a dais in his royal chair when they were ushered into his presence.

"What have you done to me this time?" he asked in Egyptian.

Judah spoke, broken by his anguish. "What can we say to my lord?" he said. "God has found out the guilt of your servants, and we shall be your slaves. All of us."

"No," said Joseph. "Not all of you. Only him whose sack had my silver cup. Him. The rest can go home to your father."

Judah's face twisted with grief. Joseph set his jaw. Judah crept toward him then bowed to the floor. "O my lord," he said, "let not your anger burn against your servant for speaking."

Joseph stiffened. He was fighting tears.

But Judah flinched in fear. He gathered strength and spoke nonetheless. "The first time we came, you asked about our father. We told you the truth: he is old. He has already lost one son. He will die if he must lose another. Especially his youngest son, Benjamin. But that is the one you demanded to see."

Joseph raised his face and shut his eyes tight.

Judah said, "Our father begged us not to bring the lad here to you. He said that any harm to Benjamin would bring his grey head down to death, because Benjamin's mother had two sons and one is gone. But you demanded it, my lord, so I argued hard for Benjamin's coming. I vowed to bear the blame of any trouble. I took an oath. Therefore, I beg you, let me stay in my brother's stead. Take me, not him. How can I go back to my father if his son is not with me? What could I say? I cannot. I cannot."

Joseph could not control himself anymore.

In Egyptian he whispered, "Get out! Everyone but the Hebrews, leave the room."

When they were alone, he looked at his brothers and burst into tears. He knelt down in front of Judah and embraced him. In Hebrew he said, "Brother, didn't you know?"

He stood up and went to Benjamin and kissed him. "I am Joseph," he said.

"Reuben," he sobbed. "Reuben, look at me. Simeon, I am your brother. Levi, look, I am not dead. I did not die. I'm alive. It's me. Dan! Asher! Gad! Naphtali—it's me, Joseph!"

One after the other, he fell on the necks of his brothers and held them close until all the men were weeping.

"I have been in the hands of God from the time you took me from my father. Oh, my father! Please! Go to my father! Tell him who I am. Tell him Egypt is prepared to receive him in a royal glory. Issachar! Zebulun, run to our father and bring him here, to live the rest of his days in peace, with me, with us, with his whole family surrounding his tent all the days of his life."

6

And so it happened that Jacob and his children and their children and all their goods moved south and west into the land of Goshen, where Joseph came in a splendid chariot to meet his father.

Joseph leaped from the chariot.

Jacob limped toward him, an old man with a thin white beard. Each man fell on the neck of the other.

Old Jacob said, "Now let me die, since I have seen your face and know that you are alive."

But he lived yet twelve more years. And before he died, he blessed his children, as well as the two sons of Joseph, Ephraim and Manasseh.

Then he drew his feet up into his bed and breathed his last.

But ages later, when God had fulfilled his promises and had made the family of Abraham and Isaac and Jacob multitudinous and strong; centuries later, when the Lord had led the children of Israel out of Egypt and back to the land he had covenanted to give them, they remembered their father with a creed repeated at every harvest, and thus did they give thanks unto their faithful God.

They said:

A wandering Aramaean was my father;
    he went down to Egypt and sojourned there,
        few in number,
but there he became a nation,
    great and mighty and many.
And the Egyptians treated us harshly . . .

INTERLUDE

✢

1

Even so did the family of Abraham and of Isaac and of Jacob begin. Even so were they led by God into Egypt and into glory for a little while. A very brief while. "The Children of Israel" they would call themselves, remembering the name which God had conferred upon their ancestor Jacob.

But the Egyptians called them the "Hebrews," those who lived at the edges of civilization.

And in the centuries that followed, the kings of Egypt feared the Hebrews because they multiplied so massively. The seventy who had at first traveled into Egypt had grown over the centuries into more than six hundred thousand men. Add to that their women and their children, and one can see why the kings of Egypt strove to break the spirits of this outcast people, forcing them to labor under circumstances both cruel and dishonorable.

But God had not forgotten them. The God of Abraham and of Isaac and of Jacob remembered the children and descended like a hero on their behalf.

2

There is a portion of the Book of Genesis which we have not yet told: the first eleven chapters, the primordial history, the narratives of Creation and of the Fall, of the Flood and of the Tower of Babel.

We have withheld these stories because they carried a greater, more ancient weight when they were told aloud to families gathered in the night. Abraham was the father of a particular nation: of Israel, the Jews. Abraham and Isaac and Jacob were plucked from among all the peoples of earth to be blessed particularly, the elect of God, who gave them his name: I WILL BE WHAT I WILL BE.

But why God should choose a single people in the first place; why this became the route by which a merciful God would enter creation in order to manifest his power, his will, and his salvation—*that* story embraces all the peoples on earth everywhere and in all time.

The First Stories, then, are not exclusive to a certain people. The First Stories reveal Israel's God to be God of all the cosmos, even as they reveal Israel herself to be all the more honored for having been chosen by such a God.

The First Stories put Israel into the context of the whole world, all time and all space.

They were told with a peculiar awe.

They were *told*: uttered out loud in the hearing of gathered peoples all sitting on the ground. And they were received, likewise, in the peculiar silences of reverence.

Bere'shith . . .

In the beginning, God . . .

They had the great weight of age upon them. They tolled like the enormous bells of the universe: BONG!— establishing time, both the seasons and the days; BONG!—fixing a congenial, livable space beneath a protective firmament and upon dry ground; BONG!—declaring the supremacy of God, since everything that came to be had come to be as the utterance of the Deity himself; BONG!—creating humanity, all humanity, as unique among living things, creating humanity in the Holy Self's Image, then granting that same humanity dominion in the world, as if people were the signature of God graven ever upon his wonderful conceiving: we, the flourish of the Lord God upon creation.

BONG, BONG, BONG, until humanity sinned and separated itself, therefore, from the Deity, so that the mighty God had to conceive new ways by which to draw the world unto himself again.

The First Stories, the Stories of First Things, the Primordial narratives—when did Israel develop the vision and the courage to tell them without shrinking from them?

3

The God of Abraham and of Isaac and of Jacob raised up a prophet to speak on his behalf before the King of Egypt and all the powers of the earth. With signs and mighty wonders, Moses led the Children of Israel out of Egypt, into the wilderness, even unto the Holy Mountain where God himself descended to establish a covenant with this people from among all the peoples.

At Sinai he spoke in strength and smoke, and Moses brought his word to the people. That word defined the relationship which God offered Israel. It presented the Law whereby Israel should live thereafter, signs that this people was God's peculiar people.

By that word they constructed the Tabernacle.

By that word they traveled the wilderness until they were brought to the eastern edge of the Jordan River, where Moses in his one hundred and twentieth year recalled for them all that God had done.

Did Moses then for the first time utter the most ancient of stories? The primordial tales of creation and sin, of a disappointed God who washed the world in flood, and a merciful God who gently restored humanity to the earth again?

They were a young people still. Perhaps a young people, filled with ebullience, a teenage nation trembling to enter a new land and to take it for themselves—perhaps those who looked forward much more easily than they did backward would have heard the ancient tales but lightly. Glory was before them, not behind. Under Joshua, they lunged into the land, Canaan.

4

After the Children of Israel had settled in the Promised Land—accomplishing a remarkable transformation, turning themselves from nomadic tribes into farmers and herders—what stories did they tell to define themselves?

For the next two hundred years they repeated a sorry pattern over and over, as if it were a wheel rolling. First they would forget the laws which God had given them at Sinai: they turned away from their protective God without whom, second, they would be attacked by one of their enemies. Thus the wheel rolled a quarter and a quarter. Feeling the suffering and the oppression of their enemies, the children (third) remembered God and cried out unto him for deliverance. And every time they repented, every time they cried for help to the Lord God, he returned to them. The fourth quarter of the wheel's rolling always belonged to God, who would inspire a single Israelite with such force and charisma that this one, as "Judge," would lead Israel to victory against the enemy.

Thus a full round of the wheel. But thus it rolled through its revolutions again and again. And the Judges who God raised up in succession were these: Othniel, Ehud, and Shamgar; Deborah of wise might; Gideon completely dependent upon God; Tola and Jair and Jephthah, who caused his own daughter to die as a sacrifice;

Ibzan, Elon, and Abdon; finally, Samson, the slayer of many Philistines.

The Judges acted rather more than they talked, though some had the tongue of God in their mouths. Deborah: did she, who could sing powerful poetry in praise to God, perhaps recount the ancient tales while she sat beneath the palm tree between Ramah and Bethel? Would this have alerted a sinful people to the depth of their sin, defined by the height of their God?

Language from Deborah's mouth came forth like wind and rain and lightning. Surely, no one could have listened to her telling of the Flood without gasping for breath above torrents, the onrushing torrents, sweeping them away.

5

Or did the most serious telling of the Primordial Stories await the coming of Kings to Israel?

After Samson had died in a pagan temple—bringing down the stone walls upon his own head and upon two thousand helpless Philistines—Israel began to demand a king to rule over them.

The last Judge to lead Israel with righteousness and wisdom, a Priest of perfect obedience and, at the same time, a reliable prophet of God, was Samuel the son of Elkanah and of Hannah, his mother. There was in those days no one like Samuel, in communication with the Lord God.

When he had grown very old, the elders of Israel came to him at Ramah and said, "Behold, you are old and your sons do not walk in your ways; now appoint for us a king to govern us like all the nations."

Samuel relented, though he feared what a king might do to this people. So much power in one hand—

if it is not directed by the Lord God in faithfulness and obedience—could undermine a nation, could ultimately destroy it.

Samuel anointed two men in succession as kings of Israel. The first was Saul of the tribe of Benjamin, for whom the office grew too heavy to bear. The second was David of the tribe of Judah, a man of remarkable skill, for whom the crown was a light and splendid fit. Saul died on the battlefield. David died an old man in his bed, having extended his kingdom north and east and south farther than a single and united Israel would ever stretch again.

Unto David did Samuel utter warnings regarding pride and power? Did the old man train the young one by recounting with some passion the first sins of the world and the consequences of these?

Ah, the language of the Primordial Stories—especially the tales of Adam and Eve, of Cain and Abel, of the pride of the people of Babel—is so much like the language of David's day that surely someone set this Triumphant King David with the Context of All Existence. Someone made him alert to the First Things of God. Maybe that someone was Nathan, the prophet who called David to account for his blood-lusty sins against Bathsheba and her husband, Uriah the Hittite.

> For David did return unto God aware of his
>   transgression:
> Against thee, thee only, have I sinned
>   And done this evil in thy sight:
> that thou mightest be justified when thou speakest,
>   and be clear when thou judgest.

For God made a covenant with David, even as he had made a covenant with all the Children of Israel at

Mount Sinai. And in both cases God declared that the covenant would last as long as the Other—whether these were the descendants of Jacob altogether or the descendants of David in particular—remained faithful unto him, unto the Lord God.

Surely someone continued to utter the grave tales of the First Things even after David had died peacefully in his old age. And someone wrote them down—again, in the same language as that in which the court records of the King were preserved.

But as the kings came and went there seemed no final unity in response to the blessed memorials which God had left among his people. For some kings would listen and obey, but others would ignore the grand tapestry of God's actions and desires, instead taking upon themselves overweening pride, or in fear submitting themselves to other kings and other gods.

Who gave voice to the tales of God?

The Prophets.

For four centuries after David, the Prophets tried to call both Israel and Judah to righteousness, always reminding them of the glorious history of the Lord. These are those who strung the whole story together, for they recognized God to be a God of *history*, revealing himself in the events of humankind.

Surely, the Prophets wove the Ancient tales of Creation—

> —to the election tales of Abraham, Isaac, and Jacob—
> —to the Covenantal tales of Moses and Sinai—
> —to the present events of rebellion—
> —and return—
> —and rebellion again.

Within the context of the old tales, the Prophets defined the present day. For God would again judge as he had judged before: *They shall return to Egypt!*

Or else God would repent of judgment and in mercy make Israel into his child again: *How can I give you up?*

Yet, even as the stories of old—and the Prophets' present telling of them—predicted, first came the judgment.

And then came mercy.

6

Some two hundred years after the days of King David, the northern half of his kingdom, Israel, was destroyed by the Assyrians. These people, having forgotten their God, were scattered abroad. With no story to hold them together, with no spiritually cohesive force, they vanished from the earth and from its history.

When the Lord God had been denied, the story died within them; and people without a story are like beggars without a name. Those who know not whence they come cannot know where they are going, nor who they are in the fierce demanding interim, the glare of the eternal NOW.

Again, more than three hundred years after the death of David, the southern half of his kingdom, Judah, also suffered a complete defeat by the armies of the Babylonians.

But when this people was removed from their land, from Jerusalem and the Temple before which they had encountered God, and when they were driven into exile, they took the stories with them!

Still in exile, they told one another the whole history of the Lord their God. In a shining, polished version even the Most Ancient of Tales was told again, was written down, was preserved for the generations yet to come: especially the story of the Sabbath, which was one law that Judah could obey *wherever* they were in the world. They did not need a temple in order to keep the Sabbath holy.

And now prophets plucked out a most tender word from the long string of old stories, which word they applied to the rough life of Judah in exile. The word in Hebrew is *hesedh*: this is the peculiar mercy of God for his people. This is a love like the love a mother feels, suffers, delights in for her child.

There arose in exile a prophet who prophesied a *repeat* of the story of Redemption which Israel had experienced in the Exodus from Egypt. Yes! In their past, Judah's present is defined. Yes! In the Story is contained the seed of their future.

Listen to this prophet combine *both* the primordial Creation Story *and* the Exodus Story in order to name the present story:

> *Awake, awake, put on strength,*
> > *O arm of Yahweh;*
> *awake as in the days of old,*
> > *the generations of long ago.*
> *Was it not thou that didst cut Rahab in pieces,*
> > *that didst pierce the dragon?*

Isaiah 51:9

This refers to the most ancient language in which creation is recounted, for "Rahab" is the dragon of darkness and chaos; it stands for "The Deep" over which the Spirit of God moved, in spite of which the Word of God caused order and light and space and time.

Was it not thou that didst dry up the sea,
*   the waters of the great deep;*
that didst make the depths of the sea a way
*   for the redeemed to pass over?*

v. 10

In the same breath, at the same holy moment, this is also the God who led Israel out of Egypt into nationhood, out of nothingness into somethingness, out of slavery into freedom and the identity as Priests of God.

This God of the Story, now, is the God who tomorrow shall bring his people home, into their own land, their own names, their own everlasting joy:

The ransomed of the Lord shall return
*   and come with singing to Zion;*
everlasting joy shall be upon their heads;
*   they shall obtain joy and gladness,*
*   and sorrow and sighing shall flee away.*

v. 11

Thus the telling of the History of the God of Creation and the God of Salvation, one God and the same, defined for the Jews in exile the joy of their sorrow.

Yes, the story was being told them.

7

And after they returned from Exile, even then the story had to be repeated, the most Ancient Tales of the First Things.

Because years went by while the people sank into deeper and deeper gloom. Those who returned had been few, and they had found the city of Jerusalem a rubble. No Temple. No walls of protection. The weather in those years ruined their efforts to raise good crops. Their enemies, both from the north in Samaria and from the south around Hebron, harassed them and kept them both poor and tired.

Early at their returning they had rebuilt a foundation for a new temple structure, but then they had quit working and struggled just to subsist.

Ah, they were a melancholy, hopeless people.

They married their daughters to Samaritans in order to elevate themselves by a little dowry.

In a grey lethargy, they forgot God.

But God did not forget them.

Through one man God inspired them to begin work on their wall again, through Nehemiah. And so the external strength of their lives began to revive.

But it took another man to revive their internal strength, their souls, and their fixed obedience unto the Lord.

This man was a Priest. He was also a storyteller.

When did Israel develop the vision and the courage to tell the most Ancient of Stories to one another without shrinking from them?

Whenever else it might have been, of this we may be sure: that Ezra read again before the people the whole Holy History, starting at the very beginning:

Bere'shith:

In the Beginning, God . . .

Part II

The Primal Stories

✽

EZRA

1

Nehemiah has no illusions concerning his accomplishments in Jerusalem—what he can and what he cannot do.

A wall is good and necessary, a weapon protecting the city against enemies from without. A wall lends courage to its citizens, strength to its warriors, peace to its merchants and priests and scholars. But it does not make a people righteous. It cannot protect against the enemy from within.

Nehemiah knows: faithlessness and disobedience destroy a nation at its root. And though a governor may build walls and organize administrations and punish misbehavior, he cannot control the heart. He cannot persuade a people to repent. The Law of God must do that.

But in Jerusalem there are no scribes who love the Law enough. And the priests lack moral force. They are as corrupt as the people. Both neglect the Sabbath with impunity.

In people such as this, a wall breeds pride and a false contentment.

So Nehemiah has written to his benefactor, Artaxerxes of Persia, with one more urgent request: "For the sake of Judah and Jerusalem, send from Babylon Ezra the priest, scribe of the Law of God. The temple here is impoverished. The Jews scarcely know their heritage or their God."

2

Eight months after he begged for Ezra's presence; five months after the king agreed and the priest organized a grand caravan of the most respected Jews in Babylon; three days after their journey's end, when the caravan disbanded in the countryside outside Jerusalem, on the morning of that day, Nehemiah stands in a fresh city gate and watches as Ezra himself approaches.

A slow, lank man with pouches under his eyes, deliberate in all his movement, Ezra walks in front of a procession of camels, all of them burdened. The priest is very tall, gazing forward like one of his camels. The nearer he comes, the more Nehemiah must tilt his head up in order to look in Ezra's face.

"You are Ezra the son of Seraiah?"

"I am," the tall priest says, pausing.

"Ezra, skilled in the law of Moses which the Lord God of Israel gave to him?"

When Ezra stops, so does the line of camels behind. "And who are you?" he says.

"Nehemiah, governor of Judah, the servant of Artaxerxes." Nehemiah puts forward his hand. "I'm the one who prayed that you would come. Welcome."

Slowly Ezra takes the smaller man's hand, his eyes resting on Nehemiah's splendid robes.

"I have a duty to discharge," the priest says. "Where is the temple?"

So Nehemiah leads the unhurried priest and twelve camels through Jerusalem up the Temple Mount. There Ezra delivers all the treasure he has brought from Babylon by order of Artaxerxes. He weighs it and records the weights: Six hundred and fifty talents of silver, silver vessels worth a hundred talents, a hundred talents of gold, twenty bowls of gold worth a thousand darics, and two vessels of fine bright bronze as precious as gold.

As the days pass, Ezra oversees a sacrifice. It takes a month. Nehemiah could have done it in a week, but he is not a priest. Ezra attends to every particular with equanimity, then reviews what he has done: he keeps an accounting. So the Jews who came with him from exile offer to God twelve bulls, ninety-six rams, seventy-seven lambs—and as a sin offering, twelve he-goats.

But if Nehemiah cannot offer sacrifices, yet he can command people.

When Ezra's sacrificing has been completed, the governor of Judah sends out a decree that all the citizens of his province must gather in Jerusalem on the first day of the seventh month of the year: men and women, all who are old enough to hear with understanding.

At the same time he orders workmen to construct a platform of new timber in the square before the Water Gate, a pulpit high enough for thousands to see a single individual standing there. And then Nehemiah meets Ezra in a private room and speaks with passion: "You must read the Book of the Law to this people," he says. He can't control the urgency in his voice. He glares into the pouchy eyes of the priest. "Read it word for word. Read it clearly— and explain it, so that the people understand it. They have forgotten Egypt and the wilderness and Mount Sinai and the words of God which Moses wrote in the law. Ezra, priest, scribe: they have forgotten covenant!"

3

It is dawn, the first day of the seventh month—a heavy, quiet dawn, though crowds of people have gathered in Jerusalem. No one is speaking.

In the square before the Water Gate, a great congregation sits on the ground facing a high, spare platform built of newly hewn wood.

Nehemiah is on the platform. He has commanded the sitting and the silence. He will wait and not grow impatient. He will present the people with a calm aspect.

But soon enough he sees Ezra the priest coming down from the old palace mount, carrying scrolls in his two arms.

While Ezra moves forward through the multitude, Nehemiah descends and goes to meet him. Hands rise around the tall priest. A woman reaches and touches one of the scrolls, then snatches her hand back and covers her mouth. An old man rises, lightly kisses the book, then sits again. And Nehemiah, when he comes face-to-face with Ezra, cannot help himself. He drops to his knees. He, too, kisses the Book of the Law, and he begins to weep. He withdraws. He will watch and listen from a distance, hiding his face and his emotion.

Ezra is followed by twelve important people of Judah. When he ascends the platform, six stand to his right and six to his left, but he is much the tallest, a gaunt chalky figure in the center slowly sweeping his gaze over all the people.

Now he unrolls the book to its beginning. Suddenly, the people rustle and begin to rise. Ezra pauses until the entire square is standing, then he lifts his arms and chants, "Deliver us, O God of our salvation! Save us from among the nations, that we may give thanks to your holy name, and glory in your praise." To the people directly, now, the priest calls in slow measured tones: "Blessed be the Lord, the God of Israel, from everlasting to everlasting!"

The people answer, "Amen!" To Nehemiah it is like the sighing of wind in cedar trees: the people lift their hands and murmur, "Amen." Then they bow their heads and worship the Lord. Ezra watches and waits.

When the whole congregation is seated on the ground again and the square is quiet, Ezra turns his eyes to the words in front of him and begins to read.

"In the beginning," he intones the holy words. "In the beginning God created the heavens and the earth."

"Ahhh," Nehemiah sighs to himself: the words.

Ezra reads with slow articulation. He finds a rhythm in the language and slowly, slowly rocks his body to the reading:

In the beginning God created the heavens and the earth.

The earth was without form. Everywhere was emptiness; everything was darkness. But the Lord sent forth his spirit as a storm on the terrible deep.

And God said, "Let there be light."

And light shined in the emptiness, and God saw that the light was good. He divided the light from the darkness. The light he called "Day." The darkness he called "Night." And when the evening and the morning had passed, that was the first day.

And God said, "Let there be a firmament in the midst of the waters to divide the wild water above from the waters below."

And it was so. God called the firmament "Heaven," and that was the end of the second day.

God said, "Let the waters under heaven flow down to the places I appoint for them that the dry ground might appear." So the waters ran in streams and rivers to the ocean. The waters obeyed their boundaries, and God called the dry land "Earth" and the greatest gathering of waters "the sea," and he said, "It is good."

Then he said, "Let the earth put forth green growing things, plants with seed and trees with fruit so that each kind can reproduce in the time to come." And it was so, and it was good—and that was the third day of the world.

God said, "Now let there be two lamps in the firmament to distinguish day from night. They shall measure the times by their shining, the years, the seasons, and the days." So God set two lamps in heaven—the greater to rule the day, the lesser to rule the night—and some stars. And he saw that it was good.

Evening and morning were the fourth day.

God said, "Let the waters swarm with living things!" God also said, "Let birds fly as high as the heavens!"—and in this manner he created the great sea monsters and the fish and every winged bird according to its kind. And God blessed them, saying, "Be fruitful and multiply: fill the waters in the seas, and the lands and the branches and the bright air of the heavens!"

That was the fifth day.

And God said, "Let the earth bring forth living creatures, cattle and crawling things and the untamed beasts." And it was so, each creature fashioned according to its kind, and God saw that it was good.

"But now," said the Lord God, "now let me make a race in my own image, after my likeness—"

So the Lord God made of red clay a human form, and into its nostrils he breathed the breath of life—and the clay came alive. It rose up on two legs and walked.

That same day the Lord planted a garden in the east, in Eden. He filled it with trees both pleasant to look at and good to eat. In the middle of the garden he placed the Tree of Life and the Tree of the Knowledge of Good and Evil. Then he brought the human to the garden and said, "Behold, I give you plants and animals, fish and fowl, green things, breathing things—everything. Govern it all. In my name, take care of it all.

"And you may eat of every tree in Eden except the one in the middle. You must never eat of the Tree of the Knowledge of Good and Evil—for in the day that you do, you shall surely die."

But when he had placed this single figure in the wide, fruitful garden, God did not say, "It is good." He considered the solitary man and said, "It is not good for anyone to be alone. I will make a helper fit for him."

So God brought him animals, to see what he would call them; and whatever the man called each creature, that was its name. But among these there was not found a helper perfectly fit for him.

So God laid the man down on a green hillock and caused a deep sleep to fall upon him; and while he slept the Lord took one of his ribs and closed up its place with flesh, and of that rib God formed a woman.

Then he woke the man and showed him the woman he had made.

The man laughed in delight and cried: "At last! Bone of my bone, flesh of my flesh!" Then, gently, he approached this second person and said, "Were you taken from man? Then you shall be called woman."

So the man and the woman lived in Eden, naked but not ashamed. And God saw everything that he had made, and behold: it was very good.

This was the end of the sixth day.

And when he had finished all his work, the heavens and the earth and the host of them, the Lord God rested. He rested on the seventh day, and he blessed that day thereby forever. Every seventh day is holy and devoted unto God.

Ezra the priest stops reading. He lifts his heavy eyes and looks to the side, seeing nothing. So elegant the words he has just read—so elemental, embracing the whole world—yet to Nehemiah it seems that the priest is bearing a burden greater than any his camels have ever borne.

How cavernous are the minds of the scribes of God! How much they carry in memory!

Suddenly Nehemiah realizes that Ezra need not read the words in order to know them. The Book of Moses lives whole within him. He sees all the words and all the laws in a single glance, as from a high mountain. And though the congregation is receiving the story sentence by sentence, for Ezra the priest every sentence contains the entire story from beginning to end.

Yet, he reads. He reads because he loves the words themselves, and to read each is to honor it.

Ezra turns to the scroll again, draws a slow breath, and continues:

Now, the serpent was more cunning than any other creature that the Lord God had made.

He said to the woman, "Did God say, 'You shall not eat of any tree in the garden'?"

The woman said, "We may eat of the fruit of the trees of the garden; but God said, 'You shall not eat of the fruit of the tree in the middle of the garden, neither shall you touch it, lest you die.'"

But the serpent said, "You will not die. For God knows that when you eat of it your eyes will be opened. You will be like God, knowing good and evil."

When, therefore, the woman considered the tree and saw that it was lovely to look at and good for food and able to make one wise, she plucked its fruit and ate. Next, she gave some to her husband, and he ate.

Immediately their eyes were opened: they saw that they were naked, and they rushed to cover themselves with aprons of fig leaves.

At dusk the man and his wife heard the sound of the Lord God walking in the garden, and they hid themselves. The Lord God called to the man, "Where are you?"

The man said, "I heard the sound of your coming, and I was afraid because I am naked, so I hid myself."

The Lord said, "Who told you that you were naked? Have you eaten of the tree from which I commanded you not to eat?"

The man said, "The woman whom you gave to me—she offered me the fruit and I ate."

Then the Lord God said to the woman, "What have you done?"

The woman said, "The serpent charmed me, and I ate."

So then, in the darkness of the night arriving, the Lord God announced to his creatures the consequences of their sins. To the serpent he said: "Hereafter you shall crawl on your belly and eat dust all the days of your life. Your seed shall be at war with the seed of the woman—and though you may strike his heel, he shall crush your head."

To the woman the Lord said: "The bearing of children shall cause you difficulty and a heavy pain. Yet you shall hunger after a husband, and he shall rule over you."

To the man he said: "Because you disobeyed my word, the very earth is cursed. It shall trouble your labor with thorns and thistles. All the days of your life you shall eat bread in toil and sweat—and in the end you shall return to the clay from which you came. Dust you are: to dust you shall return."

Then the Lord drove the man and the woman out of Eden. At the east side of the garden he set cherubim with flaming swords turned every way, flashing like lightning, to guard the gate.

The man was named Adam, after the earth. The woman was called Eve, because she was the mother of all living.

Outside Eden, Adam lay with Eve, and she conceived and bore a son. She named the child Cain. Soon she bore another son and named him Abel.

When Cain grew up, he became a farmer.

Abel became a shepherd.

In time the brothers brought sacrifices to the Lord, each according to his labor. Cain burned a smoky grain; Abel offered a sheep. And though the Lord had regard for Abel's sacrifice, for Cain's he did not.

Seeing that, Cain grew angry. His face fell into the lines of rage.

The Lord said, "Cain, why are you angry? Do well now, and it will be accepted; but if you do not, sin will be lying in wait at your door. Cain, you must master the sin!"

Nevertheless, in the months that followed, Cain kept eying his brother—and finally he said to him, "Let's go out to the fields together."

They went, and while they were there, Cain rose up and killed his brother Abel.

Then the Lord said to Cain, "Where is Abel your brother?"

He said, "How should I know? Am I my brother's keeper?"

And the Lord said, "What have you done? The voice of your brother's blood is crying to me from the ground. Therefore, Cain, the ground shall be shut against you forever. It shall no longer yield its fruit for you; but you shall be a fugitive wherever you wander on the earth."

Cain cried out, "O God, the punishment is too much for me! Because you've driven me from the soil and from your face, anyone might slay me now!"

But the Lord said, "Not so! If anyone slays Cain, vengeance shall be taken on him sevenfold."

And the Lord put a mark on Cain lest any who came upon him should kill him. And then Cain went away from the presence of the Lord and dwelt in the land of Nod, east of Eden.

Ezra the priest pauses and looks down on the people who fill the square. The longer he looks at them, the more they cannot return his gaze. They drop their eyes.

"If," says Ezra slowly, "if by resting on the seventh day the Creator blessed that day and hallowed it as a Sabbath forever, then how can you profane the day?"

No one answers him. "I have seen you treading wine presses on the Sabbath," Ezra says. "I have seen you bringing in heaps of grain and loading them on asses on the Sabbath—you sell wine, grapes, and figs on the Sabbath. Why do you do this evil thing?"

Silence. Judah is silent. Jerusalem is borne down by the priest's words—no longer a story, but a very personal sermon.

"I have just read to you the first covenant which God made with the parents of every people of the earth—the covenant which they broke by disobeying his one command. What happened at the breaking of the covenant? Life became difficult. Work became hard. The people who sinned against God also learned to sin against each other.

"The hand of a man shed the blood of his brother.

"In the ages that followed, the descendants of Adam and Eve developed new ways of living." Ezra is not reading now. He is teaching. His pouchy eyes are not judging; they are pursuing an important point. "Some people built cities. Some farmed. Some lived in tents and wandered through the wilderness with flocks and herds. People learned the arts and music. They forged instruments in copper and bronze.

"A few individuals still called on the name of the Lord. Enoch walked so closely with God that when he had lived his full number of years, God took him and he was not.

"But Enoch was unusual. Wickedness entered the world when that covenant was broken. The ground itself was cursed. People grew cunning in killing. A man named Lamech was so proud of his murders that he sang songs about them, and others learned his songs and sang them too.

"Pride prevailed in the world.

"People stole from the heavenly places powers that did not belong to them.

"In those ancient days the meditation of every human heart was evil only, evil continually, so evil that the Lord God was grieved that ever he had made the race, and he said, 'I will blot out those whom I have created from the face of the ground, people and beasts and creeping things and birds of the air, for I am sorry that I have made them.'

Again, the silence in the square before the Water Gate is a heavy one. Nehemiah had prayed for this. He was not sorry that the priest was troubling the hearts of the people—but he was sorry for his flesh, sorry to be a person at all. But then Ezra says in a softer voice, "Yet the Lord God determined to make a second covenant—to start again. Listen, Judah. Jerusalem, listen."

Now the priest bends his eyes down to the book before him and reads:

In those days one man found favor with the Lord. Noah had walked blamelessly with God for six hundred years. To Noah the Lord said: "I am going to destroy all flesh because the earth is sick with violence.

"But you, Noah: Build an ark. Make it of gopher wood four hundred and fifty feet long, seventy-five feet wide and forty-five feet high. Set a door in its side, and cover it with pitch. For I will establish my covenant with you."

Noah did what the Lord commanded. On dry land he built an ark with three levels and a roof and a door.

Then the Lord said, "Noah, go into the ark, you and your wife and your sons with their wives, too. Take with you seven pairs of every kind of clean ani-

mal and a pair of every unclean kind, the male and
its mate. Take food so that they all might live and
continue on the earth in spite of what I shall do.

"For in one week I shall send a rain by which
to blot out every living thing that I have made."

Again, Noah obeyed. Two and two, male and
female, the footed, the crawling, and the winged
creatures Noah drove into the ark. Next went his
sons Shem, Ham, and Japheth, their wives, his wife,
and finally Noah himself. Then the Lord God shut
the door.

On the seventeenth day of the second month
of the six hundredth year of Noah's life, the fountains of the terrible deep burst open and spouted
water. The wild waters above the firmament also
broke through heaven and poured down upon the
earth. For forty days and nights water roared over
the land, cataracts and waves upon the seas. The ark
rose higher and higher until the mountains themselves were covered by the flood and there was water
only, water everywhere.

All flesh perished in those days, birds and cattle, the beasts of the field and swarming things. And
people. Everyone in whom there had been breath
was drowned. Only Noah and those who were with
him survived.

After forty days the rain ceased falling. Water
continued to cover the earth. But God remembered
Noah.

He sent a strong wind across the world and the
waters began to abate.

In the seventh month the ark touched the tops
of the mountains of Ararat. Noah opened a window
and felt the breezes.

He sent forth a dove, but the dove returned to the ark and alighted in its window. She had found no place to perch.

Noah waited seven days and released the dove again. Again she came back, but this time with an olive leaf in her beak. The ark had come to rest in a cradle between two peaks of Ararat. One week later Noah released the dove a third time. She flew toward the southern sun and never came back again.

Then the Lord God said to Noah, "Open the ark. Send forth the living things that they might breed and fill the world again. And you, Noah: go forth as well. Be fruitful and multiply."

So Noah arose. He and his family went out and built an altar and offered burnt offerings to the Lord.

When the Lord smelled the pleasant odor of the sacrifice, he said, "Never again will I curse the ground. Never again will I destroy all living things. While the earth remains, seedtime and harvest, cold and heat, summer and winter, day and night shall never cease."

And God blessed Noah and his children, saying, "Every moving thing that lives shall be food for you. Only you shall not eat flesh with its life, that is, its blood. Life belongs to me. Therefore, whoever sheds human blood, by humans shall his blood be shed. For I made humankind in my own image!"

Then God said to Noah, "Behold, I establish my covenant with you and your descendants after you—that never again shall all flesh be cut off by the waters of a flood. And this is the sign of the covenant which I make between me and you for all future generations: I set my bow in the cloud. When I bring clouds over the earth and the bow is seen in them, I will remember my covenant, an everlasting covenant between God and every living creature."

In the generations after Noah, people began again to multiply. They spoke one language. Family after family, they spread eastward until they found a pleasant plain in Shinar, where they settled.

"Come," they said, "let us make bricks."

They made bricks by baking and they mortared them with bitumen. Then they said, "Let us make a city, and in its center build a tower so high it touches heaven. We will make a name for ourselves, and we will never be scattered like dust across the earth."

So the people went to work, building a monument from the plain up into the sky.

Then the Lord God came down to see what the people were doing.

"Behold," said the Lord, "they are one people speaking all one tongue, and this is only the beginning of what they will do. Soon nothing will seem impossible to them!

"Come," said the Lord, "let us confuse their language so they can't understand each other."

Therefore, the name of that city was Babel, because there the Lord confused the tongues of the people. They ceased working together, ceased building or living together. Like dust the people were scattered across the face of the whole earth.

Ezra reads, "The face of the whole earth," and immediately calls out to the Jews in the square before him: "Twice!"

He draws a deep breath. "Twice," he says, "the Creator tried to establish his covenant with the people of the world. His second covenant was with Noah and all his descendants forever--but, as at the first, the people broke this covenant, too.

"What then?

"What was next?

"What next could the Lord God do for the people he had created, who now were divided into tribes and tongues and peoples and nations?

"O Judah, don't you know? Don't you remember what the Lord has done? Israel, are you ignorant of who you are?

"Next God chose one man with whom to make his covenant—and in that man, one people!"

Nehemiah is breathless because of the sudden passion in the tall priest. Ezra has come to the goal of his sermon. He is neither weary nor indifferent now. He drops his eyes and continues reading:

When Abram was ninety-nine years old the Lord appeared to him and said, "I am God Almighty! Walk before me and be blameless. And I will make my covenant between me and you, and will multiply you exceedingly."

Then Abram fell on his face, and God said to him: "Behold, my covenant is with you. No longer shall your name be Abram, but your name shall be Abraham; for I have made you the father of a multitude of nations. I will make you exceedingly fruitful; and I will make nations of you, and kings shall come forth from you. And I will establish my covenant between me and you and your descendants after you throughout their generations for an everlasting covenant, to be God to you and to your descendants after you. And I will give to you and to your descendants after you the land of your sojournings, all the land of Canaan, for an everlasting possession; and I will be their God."

Ezra looks up.

"And who," he calls, "are the nations to come from Abraham? Can you tell me? And then can you say which nation still has that everlasting covenant? The Moabites are the children of Abraham's nephew, Lot. So are the Ammonites. Do they remember the covenant of Abraham? No.

"The Ishmaelites are children of Abraham. Do they remember the covenant? Does anyone on earth remember them?

"And Esau was one grandson of Abraham. His children are the Edomites who even today live south of us in Hebron where Abraham pitched his tent. Yet do they remember the covenant?

"Judah! With whom is the covenant?

"Abraham's other grandson was Jacob, whom God named Israel. Israel! It was with Israel that God renewed the covenant. It was Israel whom God took to himself now not as one man, but as a people, as a nation, when he delivered them from the hands of the Egyptians, where they were in bondage.

"You, Israel! Judah, you!

"For ask now of the days that are past, since the day that God created humankind upon the earth"—this time Ezra is quoting the Book of Moses from memory.

His voice is rich with the rhetoric:

"Ask from one end of heaven to the other, whether such a great thing as this was ever heard of. Has any god ever taken a nation for himself from the midst of another nation, by trials, by signs, by wonders, and by war, by a mighty hand and an outstretched arm, and by great terrors according to all that the Lord your God did for you in Egypt before your eyes? To you it was shown, that you might know that the Lord is God; there is no other besides him.

"Therefore, you must keep his statutes and his commandments, that it may go well with you, and with your children after you, and that you may prolong your days in the land which the Lord your God gives you forever.

"So, Judah," Ezra says. He whispers it. He leans forward and lowers his voice to a whisper. "So then, is it well with you, Judah? Do you possess the land your God gave unto you? No? Why not?"

Ezra continues quoting:

The Lord our God made a covenant with us at Sinai. He spoke with us face-to-face out of the midst of the fire.

He said, "I am the Lord your God, who brought you out of the land of Egypt, out of the house of bondage. You shall have no other gods before me."

The Lord said, "You shall be holy; for I the Lord your God am holy! You shall reverence your mother and your father. You shall keep my sabbaths: I am the Lord your God.

"Do not turn to idols or make for yourselves molten gods: I am the Lord your God.

"When you reap the harvest of your land, you shall not reap the field to its border. Do not strip your vineyard bare or gather the fallen grapes. These things you shall leave for the poor and the sojourner: I am the Lord your God.

"You shall not steal nor deal falsely nor lie to one another. And you shall not swear by my name falsely, profaning the name of God: I am the Lord.

"You shall not oppress your neighbors or rob them. You shall not curse the deaf or put a stumbling block before the blind, but you shall fear your God: I am the Lord.

"You shall not go up and down as a slanderer among your people: I am the Lord.

"You shall not hate a single brother or sister in your heart, but you shall reason with your neighbors, lest you bear sins because of them. You shall not take vengeance or carry grudges against the sons and daughters of your people, but you shall love your neighbors as yourself: I am the Lord."

Suddenly Ezra pauses. There is a sound in the square, very soft, like running water, and for a moment the priest is mystified. But Nehemiah, nearer the people, knows that sound. It is weeping.

The people of Judah are weeping.

No one wails. No one is crying out. The passage of sorrow through the congregation is as quiet as rainfall.

"Yes, yes," murmurs Ezra. "Now you know. The covenant is with you this day as at the first. As it was with Abraham and Isaac and Jacob; as it was with Moses at Sinai; as it was when David truly possessed the land, so it is this day still. The covenant is with you, that you might keep it again in righteousness and in purity."

But all the people continue weeping, releasing ancient griefs, centuries of sorrow:

You shall be holy, you shall be holy, you shall be holy—for I the Lord your God am holy.

Now Ezra descends from his platform. He begins to walk among the people. He touches the backs of their necks. "Hush," he says. "Don't mourn, don't weep. This day is holy to the Lord your God."

The priest moves slowly. Soon others of his entourage—the Jews, the Levites, and Nehemiah himself—are kneeling here and there among the people, comforting them.

"Go your way," says Ezra. "Eat the fat and drink sweet wine and send portions to the poor. This day is holy to our Lord. Do not be grieved, for the joy of the Lord is your strength."

It is early in the afternoon. The people rise and do as Ezra says. They eat, they drink, they send portions to those who have nothing—and soon in Jerusalem there is the beginning of consolation, because the people have understood the words that were declared to them.

So ends the reading of the first stories of the world.

Stories and People from the Bible Come to Life

The Book of God
The Bible as a Novel

Walter Wangerin Jr.

Here is the story of the Bible from beginning to end as you've never read it before. *The Book of God* reads like a fine novel, bringing a wise and beautiful rendering of the Bible, retold by master storyteller Walter Wangerin Jr.

Wangerin recreates the high drama, low comedy, gentle humor, and awesome holiness of the Bible story. Imaginative yet meticulously researched, *The Book of God* offers a sweeping history that stretches across thousands of years and hundreds of lives, in cultures foreign and yet familiar in their common humanity.

From Abraham wandering in the desert to Jesus teaching the multitudes on a Judean hillside, *The Book of God* follows the biblical story in chronological order. Priests and kings, apostles and prophets, common folk and charismatic leaders—individual stories offer glimpses into an unfolding revelation that reaches across the centuries to touch us today.

The Book of God is available at Christian bookstores near you.

The Book of God

0-310-20005-9 - Hardcover

0-310-20422-4 - Audio Tape
    unabridged dramatic reading by the author

0-310-21068-2 - Video Tape

ZondervanPublishingHouse
Grand Rapids, Michigan
http://www.zondervan.com

A Division of HarperCollinsPublishers

Mourning into Dancing

Walter Wangerin Jr.

"Why art thou cast down, O my soul?"

Like the psalmist, we all experience sadness, sorrow, grief. But do we always recognize the source of our grief? In *Mourning into Dancing*, Walter Wangerin Jr. defines our grief for what it is: our human response to the dozens of daily losses that afflict us. Separation, distance, loss of friends and family, loss of cherished hopes and dreams, loss of all the little things that give meaning to our lives. Ultimately, these things are like "little deaths" that come to us each day.

But herein is our hope, because to define these many losses, these "little deaths," we also must recognize what life is. It is found in our relationships with ourselves, with our world, with other people, and with our Creator. This is the dancing that can come out of mourning: the hope of restored relationships.

Mourning into Dancing defines the stages of grief, names the many kinds of loss we suffer, shows how to help the grief-stricken, gives a new vision of Christ's sacrifice, and shows how a loving God shares our grief. We learn from this book that the way to dancing is through the valley of mourning—that grief is a poignant reminder of the fullness of life Christ obtained for us through his resurrection.

Mourning into Dancing
0-310-54880-2 - Hardcover
0-310-20764-7 - Softcover

ZondervanPublishingHouse
Grand Rapids, Michigan
http://www.zondervan.com

A Division of HarperCollins*Publishers*

The Book of God for Children

Walter Wangerin Jr.

Previously published as *The Bible for Children*

The glorious creation of the world. The horror of the flood. The miracle of Exodus. The drama of David's fight against Goliath. And the wonder of Christ's birth, all in a single story.

These timeless stories come alive under the pen of master storyteller Walter Wangerin Jr. Long considered a classic among children's Bible storybooks, **The Book of God for Children** served as Wangerin's training and inspiration for writing the best-selling **Book of God**, a novelization of the Bible for adults.

Now new generations of parents and children can enjoy the whole story of the Bible told for children. So look. Listen. Read. And grow. Because God's book was written for you—God's children.

The Book of God for Children
0-310-21418-1 - Hardcover

ZondervanPublishingHouse
Grand Rapids, Michigan
http://www.zondervan.com

A Division of HarperCollinsPublishers

Winner of the ECPA Gold Medallion Award 1993

Reliving the Passion

Walter Wangerin Jr.

40 Steps to the Day of the Resurrection of Our Lord!

What a Journey! Ash Wednesday to Bethany. Gethsemane to the High Priest's House. Praetorium to Golgotha, and finally the Garden of the Tombs. No story has more significance than the death and resurrection of Jesus. Christ's Passion is a story with which we are all familiar; a significant story, but one that may have lost much of its meaning through repetition. Now, by following the forty meditations outlined in this book, we can truly experience the wonder and glory of Christ's Passion.

Beginning on Ash Wednesday, each day's devotion focuses on a passage from Holy Scripture, enabling us to follow the wondrous story as given in the Gospel of Mark. After walking with and learning from Jesus and experiencing the love of the Lord in His passion, our very personal journey ends with a truly joyous Easter celebration of life, faith, and Resurrection. Pick up your copy of *Reliving the Passion* at Christian bookstores near you.

Reliving the Passion

0-310-75530-1 - Hardcover

0-310-21499-8 - Mass Market

ZondervanPublishingHouse

Grand Rapids, Michigan

http://www.zondervan.com

A Division of HarperCollinsPublishers

Little Lamb, Who Made Thee?

Walter Wangerin Jr.

Growing up is hard—at any age. The stories and essays in *Little Lamb, Who Made Thee?* by award-winning author Walter Wangerin Jr. portray children, teenagers, adults, and parents as they grapple with the deep realities of life. And at the heart of this struggle are the vital relationships we have with our families, for it is from our parents—and from our children—that we most profoundly learn about ourselves as children of God.

Through personal reminiscences as a child, minister, and parent, Walter Wangerin helps us see our world anew. His sage advice and joyful humor are couched in vivid stories—warm and intimate, raucous and poignant—that are his trademarks. He gets inside his subject and reveals the wonderful open secret that parenthood and childhood are the great, miraculous, and profound mysteries of our lives. In *Little Lamb, Who Made Thee?* Walter Wangerin shares his touching insights in a unique and unforgettable way.

Little Lamb, Who Made Thee?

0-310-40550-5 - Hardcover

0-310-21483-1 - Mass Market

ZondervanPublishingHouse
Grand Rapids, Michigan
http://www.zondervan.com

A Division of HarperCollinsPublishers

We want to hear from you.
Please send your comments about this book
to us in care of the address below. Thank you.

ZondervanPublishingHouse
Grand Rapids, Michigan 49530
http://www.zondervan.com